I0589008

on Wings of Song

Anne Barwell

Copyright © 2020 Anne Barwell

All rights reserved. No part of this story may be used, reproduced, or transmitted in any form or by any means without written permission of the copyright holder, except in the case of brief quotations embodied within critical reviews and articles.

This book is a work of fiction. All names, characters, places, and events are products of the writer's imagination or have been used factiously and are not to be construed as real. Any resemblance to persons, living or dead, actual events, locale, or organisations is entirely coincidental.

Published by LaceDragon Publishing

All trademarks, brands, and or licensed materials mentioned are registered trademarks of their respective holders/companies.

Cover design: © 2014 T.L. Bland
Publishing logo © 2019 T.L. Bland
http://www.thruterryseyes.com/
Cover art is for illustrative purposes only and any person depicted on the cover is a model

Editing: Desi Chapman
Blue Ink Editing
https://blueinkediting.com/

ISBN: 978-0-473-51624-6 (epub)

ISBN: 978-0-473-51625-3 (mobi)
ISBN: 978-0-473-51623-9 (print)

First Edition published by Dreamspinner Press, 2014

AUTHOR'S NOTE

Although this story is a work of fiction, it is set against a backdrop of actual places and events. While many of the locations used in this story are real, some liberties have been taken for the sake of a good story.

ALSO BY ANNE BARWELL

FROM LACEDRAGON PUBLISHING

Slow Dreaming

Co-written with Lou Sylvre

From JMS Books

Sunset at Pencarrow

DEDICATION

In memory of all those who fought in WW I. Lest we forget.

ACKNOWLEDGMENTS

A huge thanks to everyone who convinced me to enter the world of Indie publishing, and supported me through the whole process. A special thanks to the New Zealand Rainbow Romance Writers group—you guys rock.

N.R. Walker for offering to format for me, and going above and beyond.

T.L. Bland for capturing Jochen and Aiden, and the feel of the story with her wonderful cover art.

Desi for editing.

Susanne, for beta reading and all her help with the German; Reesha for beta reading and wanting more of these guys; and Angela, Calli, and Sharon for beta reading.

To my writing and reading communities for your support and friendship, in particular RWNZ, and my Facebook groups Anne's Books and Brews, and Kiwi Authors Rainbow Readers.

To my family. Love you

And last, but in no way least my friends at Upper Hutt Science Fiction Club and Hutt City Libraries.

CHAPTER ONE

Jochen Weber pulled his greatcoat around him and continued watching the scene in front of him. It had snowed the night before, the ground a blanket of white, a refuge for those who had survived the last few days. Stark contrast to the devastation of clay, mud, and ruined brick that lay beneath.

Men who had shot at each other mere hours before now kicked a ball around a supposed no man's land—the forbidden area between their trenches and those of the enemy. The lines between friend and enemy had blurred: British, German, and French soldiers spent Christmas together in Flanders in Belgium.

"Come join us, Jochen!" Arndt Dahl yelled. "Put your book down."

Jochen waved but didn't move. "I haven't even started reading it," he muttered. Reading was more appealing than the game. He'd never really understood why men felt the need to kick a ball around, and preferred to lose himself in the words that came alive on the page.

He caught a movement from the corner of his eye and

turned. A young Englishman stood about a metre away, watching Jochen with something akin to curiosity. He didn't look much older than Jochen, who was barely twenty. The private, like himself—Jochen recognized the British insignia —was several centimetres taller than Jochen, with dark hair and the most amazing dark brown eyes. He smiled shyly, and Jochen couldn't help but return the gesture.

"*Frohe Weihnachten*," Jochen said quietly, not sure what else to say. "I mean, Merry Christmas."

"Merry Christmas." The man's voice had a musical quality to it, strong but not as deep as Jochen expected. "I thought this war would be over and we'd be home by Christmas. We all did."

"Perhaps we won't be fighting for much longer?" Jochen voiced the hope he mainly kept to himself. "After all, if we can find peace at Christmas, maybe it will last. The war has only been going four months, but it feels much longer." He held out his hand. "Excuse my manners. I'm Jochen. Jochen Weber."

The man shook Jochen's hand. "Aiden Foster." Aiden shook himself as though waking from a dream. "I'm sorry. I still can't believe what's happened. We're supposed to be on opposite sides. You Jerries are nothing like I expected." He flushed bright red. "I just insulted you, didn't I?"

Jochen chuckled. "That depends on what you expected." He shrugged. "You're not what I expected either, although I didn't really believe that you Tommies were as bad as we've been told. Not if your Mr Dickens is to be believed."

"You're reading Dickens?" Aiden looked surprised. "Your English is very good." He grimaced. "Probably much better than my German."

"Thank you. There were books I wanted to read that

hadn't been translated into German. It was quite the incentive, although I've also been told I'm too impatient." Jochen tapped the side of the book in his hand. "I have read Dickens, but this is Goethe." He lowered his voice. "Reading a British author in English while in a German trench during a war against his countrymen is probably not very sensible."

"About as sensible as a Tommy and a Jerry discussing literature on what is supposed to be a battlefield?" The side of Aiden's mouth twitched.

Jochen laughed. "Exactly." He liked Aiden already. He was easy to talk to and had a good sense of humour. One of the soccer balls headed straight for them. Jochen stepped between Aiden and the ball and caught it. "The goal's that way!" he yelled, pointing to a pile of sandbags a few metres away.

"You could always come and play!" Arndt laughed. He sounded happy, more so than he'd been over the last few months. He missed home, and in particular his girlfriend, Lisel.

"Don't let me stop you, if you want to join in." Aiden watched the ball for a few moments.

"Do you want to?" Jochen asked.

Aiden shook his head. "I've never been one for football or any game really." He turned to Jochen. "But as I said, don't let that stop you."

"I'd prefer to continue our conversation." Jochen kept his voice light, but truth be known, he found Aiden rather intriguing. "Besides, this war could go on for a while, and I could not honestly pass up an opportunity to discuss Dickens."

"I'm more into Tennyson and Keats," Aiden admitted. "I've read one of Dickens's books, but never got around to the rest."

Jochen gave him a look of mock horror. "Only one? Which one?"

"*David Copperfield*. Have you read it?"

"No, I haven't been able to get my hands on a copy." Jochen studied Aiden. "So... Tennyson, hmm? Anything in particular?"

"*Idylls of the King*," Aiden said without hesitation. "A storm was coming but the winds were still. And in the wild woods of Broceliande, before an oak, so hollow, huge and old it look'd a tower of ruin'd masonwork, at Merlin's feet the wily Vivien lay." He trailed off. "That's the first stanza of 'Vivien.' It's one I keep coming back to because of the war. It's like the storm, but today the winds are still, or we wouldn't be talking like this.... Oh Lord, I'm rambling, aren't I? Sorry."

"It's fine," Jochen assured him. "You make it sound so lyrical. I've never read much in the way of British poetry in English, and the flow of it is often lost in translation."

"I like poetry." Aiden shrugged, the fire in his eyes fading a little as he retreated back into himself. "It reminds me of music, I guess."

"I've heard it described as music without... the notes." Jochen hoped that didn't sound as foolish as he was certain it did. "Are you a musician?"

"Music without the notes." Aiden sounded thoughtful. "I like that." He smiled, and his expression softened. Did he realise how breathtaking he was when he smiled? "Yes, I am a musician. I've loved music for as long as I remember."

"What do you play? I love music, although I don't play anything." Jochen's grandmother had attempted to teach him the violin. It had been a disaster, and for months afterwards their cat had taken one look at him going anywhere near the instrument, howled, and run away.

"I sing." Aiden looked a little embarrassed. He studied his boots. "I've been with the Avery Theatre for about two years. Or I was until this bloody war."

"Avery Theatre?" Jochen asked.

"In London's West End." Aiden continued to stare at the ground. "It's a music hall, so there's a bit of acting involved too."

"And the shows are focused on the snow?" Performing on stage would take a great deal of confidence. Jochen wasn't sure he'd ever be able to. Or want to.

"Huh?" Aiden looked up.

"You keep looking at the snow."

"No! I mean...." Aiden sighed. "I'm not very good at talking about myself. I hate it."

"Yet you perform on stage?" Jochen tried to imagine a confident Aiden on stage, wooing the audience.

"Yes, but that's not me. Not really. When I sing, it's not me, it's a... role." Aiden shrugged again.

"It's still you," Jochen said firmly. "Be proud of who you are, Aiden. Of what you can do, and of what you want to achieve." Those were his father's words, spoken to Jochen as a child, but he'd never forgotten them. Why was he repeating them to a man he barely knew?

"Thank you." Aiden frowned and tilted his head to the side. "There's something going on over there." He gestured to the end of the makeshift soccer field. A group of men were talking together—a mix of German, British, and French officers. "I can't hear what they're saying, though. Can you?"

Jochen strained to hear, but he couldn't make it out either. "We could always go find out," he suggested, slipping his book into the pocket of his greatcoat.

"It looks as though we won't have to," Aiden said. "They've finished talking and are coming this way."

Jochen stood to attention as his commanding officer approached. Hauptmann Grünberg was accompanied by two other men of equivalent rank—the commanding officers of the British and French troops.

"This is Captain Williams and Capitaine Brodeur," said Grünberg in English. He was a good man, and fair. His men respected him. "Given this truce, we have decided to work together to bury our dead. As you are fluent in German and English, Weber, I'm counting on you to help spread the word."

"Foster, find Mills and organize shrouds and stretcher-bearers." Williams glanced back at the barbed wire fences in front of the British trenches. "It's a chance to give our chaps and theirs a decent burial."

"Yes, sir." Aiden saluted his commanding officer, took one last look at Jochen, then headed towards the group of men socialising nearby. He spoke briefly to a red-haired man. Several others overheard and joined the conversation, offering to help.

Jochen had the same response when he approached men in his own troops. They'd all lost friends and comrades over the last few weeks, and the bodies were still lying out there, decaying under the snow.

They buried their comrades in silence. Jochen offered to dig graves for both sides. The ache in his arms took his mind off what they were doing. Not completely, yet enough to numb his emotions so he could pretend he was able to ignore them. Until now, he'd known logically these men were dead, but seeing their sightless eyes and still bodies, often with limbs missing or at odd angles, made him shiver. He'd have nightmares about it soon enough.

He leaned on his shovel and closed his eyes for a moment. A light touch on his shoulder jerked him back to attention.

"It's not easy, is it?" Aiden said softly. He nodded towards the grave Jochen had just dug. Jochen realised the man in it was a British soldier. He'd dug so many graves he'd lost track of what side they'd been on. They'd all worked together to get the job done.

"It's not meant to be." Jochen watched the plain wooden cross being hammered into the ground. Someone had made crosses from old biscuit boxes. Others had taken it upon themselves to collect identity discs from the corpses so their families could be informed. "Did you know him?"

Aiden shook his head. "No. There are so many men I didn't get the chance to know. And so many I did know who are now dead." His voice shook. "We've lost so many already. How many more deaths will there be before this bloody war is over?"

"Too many." Jochen picked up his shovel. They finally seemed to be getting to the end of the burials, at least for now. These men would have the luxury of a grave, but how many more would not?

"I'm not sure who wins a war." Aiden glanced around, his gaze resting briefly on Captain Williams, who was far enough away so their conversation wouldn't be overheard. He lowered his voice. "Why are we fighting, Jochen? I joined up because it was supposed to be the right thing to do. I was going to do my bit for king and country, and save Britain from you Jerries."

"I'm thinking the same thing," Jochen admitted. "I...."

He swallowed and gripped the handle of his shovel tightly, his knuckles white. "Have you seen a man caught on the wire?"

It was an image he'd never get out of his mind. The soldier was younger than Jochen by a few months. They'd chatted briefly when Jochen had joined their unit. Conrad had been a student at Göttingen University, studying literature, so they'd had that in common. He'd had fire in his eyes when he'd spoken of his love for the subject, of his dreams for his future. An hour into the attack on Ypres he was dead. Hanging on the wire, unable to get free while shells rained down around him. Caught in the crossfire, the lower half of his body blown away a few moments later.

Jochen had vomited when he'd seen it—what was left of Conrad wasn't really him. Jochen couldn't believe it was. He didn't want to. His stomach still churned at the memory of it. He'd wanted to run at the time, to pretend the whole thing was just some kind of sick nightmare, a landscape of death brought on by something dark lingering deep in his own mind.

It wasn't.

"I've seen it," Aiden said quietly. "I wish to God I hadn't." He looked directly at Jochen. Jochen met Aiden's gaze. He'd seen an echo of Conrad's fire in Aiden when he'd talked about his music earlier that afternoon.

"Don't die on the wire, Aiden."

"I'll try not to." Aiden's words were an empty promise. They both knew it, but what else was he going to say?

The red-haired man Aiden had spoken to about arranging the burials walked over to him. He too held a shovel, and he wiped perspiration from his brow despite the cold. "There's going to be a combined service for the dead," he told them. "In about ten minutes in no man's land in front of the French trenches."

As they made their way over, men were already beginning to gather, soldiers from opposite sides sitting together, conversation dwindling to a respectful silence. A British chaplain stood in front of them, a Bible in his hand, a German beside him. Jochen recognised him, although he didn't know his name. The young man was only a few years older than Jochen and was studying for the ministry—would he ever get the chance to complete those studies?

Jochen and Aiden found somewhere to sit a few rows back from the front and joined the company of men. The German spoke first. *"Vater unser, der du bist im Himmel. Geheiligt werde dein Name."*

The British chaplain repeated the words in English. "Our Father who art in Heaven, Hallowed be thy Name."

They then spoke a few words each, some from the Bible, the rest from their hearts. Their congregation was silent apart from a few quiet "amens." Jochen saw a couple of men wipe tears away. He was close to it himself.

Finally the chaplain bowed his head in prayer. When he'd finished, he spoke quietly to the man who had come to stand next to him. It was Captain Williams. He nodded and looked over the crowd, his gaze fixing on Aiden.

Aiden must have guessed what Williams wanted. He inclined his head in response and then stood. Jochen glanced between the two men, confused. What did Williams expect Aiden to do?

"Aiden?" Jochen asked softly.

Aiden smiled at him and began to sing. "O Holy Night, the stars are brightly shining...." He lifted his head, his voice strong and clear, each note building on the last to create something truly beautiful, something angelic. Aiden's eyes shone; his body swayed slightly in time with the music. He *was* the music.

His audience sat in awe. Jochen could feel the emotion rippling through the men around him, tangible, as though he could reach out and touch it. He felt something inside himself reach out, wanting to be a part of it, to be carried along the wave of pure music, to grab it and never let go.

Finally, Aiden sang the final verse, the notes fading as he came back to himself and sat down again next to Jochen. There was no applause, it wouldn't have been appropriate, but Jochen could see men around them wiping tears. One man closed his eyes and gently moved from side to side as though he could still hear Aiden's song.

Several minutes later, the congregation dispersed, heading back to their own trenches. Aiden began to stand. Jochen laid a hand on his arm. "Can we talk?" he asked. Tomorrow they'd probably be fighting again. He'd heard whisperings that the Staff were visiting the trenches that evening, that they weren't impressed with the fraternisation between their men and those of their enemies. But Jochen didn't want to lose this magic, this brief friendship with Aiden, just yet.

"Of course." Aiden seemed surprised at Jochen's words. "What about?" He acted as though his performance hadn't happened. He was merely a soldier, nothing more.

Jochen led Aiden back to where they'd first met. Men were still talking quietly in small groups, just as reluctant to return to the reality of the war as Jochen was.

"Your singing...," Jochen said. "It was beautiful. It touched me, Aiden, took me away from everything."

Aiden blushed. "It... it was nothing."

Darkness was falling quickly. They didn't have much

time. "I wish we weren't on opposite sides," Jochen said. "I'd... perhaps in another life we would have been friends."

"I would have liked that." Aiden's blush grew deeper. He swallowed. "Perhaps we are now, just for this day. I've never met anyone who listened to me the way you do. Not my music, but me." His voice dropped to a whisper. "Thank you."

"I've never met anyone who listened to me like you do either," Jochen said. It figured, didn't it? He'd finally met someone who understood, and it had to be a man he'd probably never see again. "I'll take your song with me too. I doubt I'll ever forget it."

"What will you do after the war?" Aiden asked.

"Go back to my studies, I hope." Jochen noticed Aiden spoke of a life after the war as though they'd both have one. "I want to teach, if I can. Will you return to the theatre?"

Aiden nodded. "Yes. It's my life, really. I don't have anywhere else to go."

"You should," Jochen said. "Go back to it, I mean. People need music in their lives, especially music like yours."

In the distance lanterns were being lit. Christmas trees' lights shone from the top of the German trenches—a glimmer of home. They were all far from home tonight.

Jochen hesitated. He didn't want to say goodbye, to just walk away as though they'd never met. An idea struck him, a foolish one perhaps, but what else was there? He yanked off a button from his uniform, low down where it wouldn't be immediately noticed. "Happy Christmas, Aiden," he said, handing it to Aiden.

Aiden took it, their fingers brushing momentarily. A welcome warmth spread through Jochen. "Thank you." Aiden studied the button. "It's different to ours," he said. "A lion holding a shield. I like that." He slid it into his pocket, then pulled one off his own uniform. "Happy Christmas, Jochen."

"Thank you." Jochen took the button Aiden offered. "You're right. It is different." It was inscribed with a crown, although made of brass like his. "I'll keep it safe. I promise."

"I'll keep yours safe too," Aiden said. "I promise." He shoved his hands into his pockets. "Bloody war," he said suddenly. "I don't want to fight you, Jochen." His voice shook. "Survive this insanity, and have a good life."

Before Jochen could answer, Aiden spun on his heel and walked away. Jochen watched him go—back to the British trench, to the reality of death and killing, further away from the sanctuary of his music, leaving behind a friendship that had been doomed before it had begun.

"I don't want to fight you either," Jochen said softly. He fingered the button in his pocket. "Survive this insanity, and have a good life too, Aiden. I won't forget this. Or you."

CHAPTER TWO

So much for being home by Christmas.

Aiden shook his head in disgust. Nearly two years later and the war still showed no sign of ending. Sure, there was talk that this latest offensive would turn the tide, but he'd heard that before. Tomorrow it would be a new month—July 1916—and he was still in France, although this time in Pozières Village, in an area called the Somme.

Either side of him men slept soundly, blankets pulled around them, heads resting on the inside walls of the trench. He didn't know how they could, with the offensive planned for the morning.

Careful not to disturb his comrades, Aiden stood and stretched. He couldn't sleep. Perhaps he'd walk around a bit and see if that helped. Not that he had anywhere to go apart from following the narrow walkway of the trench. He heard voices a short distance away. Apparently he wasn't the only one unable to sleep.

The boards creaked beneath his feet. He hated those boards, but they were better than plodding through the mud underneath. One of the soldiers on sentry duty turned as he approached. "Evening, Foster," he said. "Can't sleep?"

Dusk hadn't long fallen, but they'd all learned to snatch sleep whenever they could. The evening was quiet, but that didn't mean they could safely leave the trench. Many a new arrival made the mistake of taking a peek over the parapet only to become a target of an enemy sniper.

"No." Aiden shrugged. "How long do you have left before you're relieved?"

"Another hour." Thompson jerked his head in the direction of Fenchurch Street. While common practice to use British street names for the different parts of the trench—to give a sense of the familiar—for Aiden it served as a reminder he was far from home. "Vaughan passed by about ten minutes before you did. He was talking about boiling some water for tea."

"I'll go join him. I could do with some tea. Thanks, Thompson." Aiden gave Thompson a nod and kept walking.

By the time he caught up with Stephen Vaughan, the bucket-fire was already hot and the water beginning to boil. Stephen glanced up as Aiden approached. "I swear every time I make tea I look up and you're there. How do you do it?"

Aiden chuckled and sat down next to Stephen. They'd met last October at Loos. It was the first time the British had used gas, and the wind had blown it back towards them. Stephen and Aiden had helped each other to safety and been friends ever since. He was a decent chap and had worked as a bank clerk in London before the war.

"It's a gift." Aiden noticed two mugs were already by the bucket-fire. "Surely you weren't expecting me?"

"The second mug is for me," a familiar voice said from

behind them. Aiden turned to see Lt Hawthorne, their commanding officer, approaching. "I asked Ste—Corporal Vaughan to make me one as he was already boiling the water for tea." Hawthorne sat down opposite Stephen. "Carry on with your conversation and don't mind me. Do you want me to grab another mug?"

"Good evening, sir. I can get the extra mug. After all, I'm the uninvited guest here." Aiden liked and respected Hawthorne. He was about the same age as Aiden and Stephen, but upper-class men tended to become officers rather than enlisted soldiers. Some seemed to have the attitude that their class meant they were superior, but Hawthorne didn't. He mucked in and did what he expected his men to do, and they respected him for it.

"No, those would be the rats," Hawthorne said dryly. "Stay there, Foster. I'll get it." He disappeared around the corner into another trench. It led to the officers' dugout.

Stephen watched him go, then seemed to realise what he was doing and pulled himself up.

"Am I intruding?" Aiden asked. He'd noticed Stephen and Hawthorne had struck up a friendship of sorts. Often men met during war who wouldn't have usually. Or formed friendships that would never have happened off the battlefield, let alone on it. A friendship between an enlisted man and an officer was as unlikely as one between two soldiers on opposing sides. And just as frowned upon. Stephen knew about the truce back in Christmas 1914, which was one of the reasons he trusted Aiden to keep his own secret.

Aiden fingered the button he wore with his identity disc around his neck. Jochen's button.

Was Jochen still alive? Aiden hoped so. Sometimes, when he had a quiet moment to himself, he closed his eyes and imagined Jochen settled in a corner of one of the

German trenches, reading. Not Dickens, as that wouldn't be appropriate, but the Goethe book he'd been carrying when they'd met. Or perhaps a work by some other German author. Aiden didn't know much about German literature. After the war he intended to do something about that.

He'd enjoyed those few hours with Jochen. He went back to it, reliving it, when he needed somewhere in his mind in which to retreat from the war. Jochen was soft-spoken, and when he'd listened to what Aiden had to say, he'd really listened, and understood. His eyes had reminded Aiden of the blue of the sky on a clear summer's day.

"No, you're not intruding," Stephen said. "Privacy is a luxury none of us have in these trenches. I can't wait to get out of here. I have a week in one of the support trenches after this and then two weeks' rest."

"I'm looking forward to sleeping in a proper bed," Aiden admitted.

"I've forgotten what a decent mattress feels like." Stephen glanced up when Hawthorne approached. He smiled. "A decent mattress and a good night's sleep."

"You're talking about your mattress dreams again?" Hawthorne chuckled. "I swear you're fixated on them." Given his response, Stephen must have told him Aiden knew about their friendship.

"At least you get a stretcher, being an officer," Stephen said. "Sir."

"I can assure you it's not comfortable." Hawthorne poured himself a mug of tea and sipped it slowly. He stretched out his legs. "I'd be happy with a hot bath. I keep telling myself I should be more disturbed than I am with the realisation that I can no longer smell the stench I could when I arrived."

"That's probably because you're now a part of it," Stephen said with a straight face.

"Thank you for that revelation." Hawthorne poured another mug of tea and handed it to Stephen. Their fingers brushed briefly, and Aiden could have sworn their touch lingered. "Here, it should be muddy enough for you now."

No, it was definitely his imagination. He'd been thinking of Jochen, and that moment between them kept replaying in his mind.

He wished they'd had more time to become friends. Watching Stephen and Hawthorne interacting brought it home. Although Aiden thought of Stephen as a good friend, it wasn't the same as what he'd felt for Jochen. If he could only work out what it was he *had* felt that day.

"Thanks, Simon." Stephen sipped his tea. "Are you nervous about tomorrow's offensive, Aiden? I'm bloody terrified."

"Bloody terrified about describes it." Aiden helped himself to tea. Like Stephen, he preferred his to steep awhile before drinking it. "I still have nightmares about Loos and that gas." He'd wake up sometimes gasping for breath, sure he'd been caught in another attack. The attack itself wasn't what drove his dreams, but the stories he'd heard about what it could do to a fellow, the damage it could do to lungs and vocal cords. Although he hadn't sung for months, he still clung to his music like a life raft. Without it, he was nothing.

Stephen shuddered. "I wouldn't be here if it wasn't for you. I'm never going to get used to any of this. I see some of the other chaps, and I wonder how they harden themselves to all this death."

"I doubt they actually do," Hawthorne said. "Just because a man doesn't show how he's feeling doesn't mean he's not feeling it." His long fingers curled around his mug. "Stiff upper lip and all that."

"I'm not sure that's a good thing," Aiden said. He'd seen his own father cry on occasion, but not when he thought his son was watching. When he'd left for the front, his father had hugged him roughly and told him he loved him. It wasn't a sentiment he voiced often.

"It's not." Hawthorne studied Stephen and Aiden for a moment. "You two could be brothers, you know." Hawthorne was fairer in comparison, his hair a lighter shade of brown, as were his eyes.

Stephen laughed. "We've been told that before, although we're definitely not." He grinned. "Besides, I have the better sense of humour."

"Of course you have." Aiden recognized the banter for what it was. It was a retreat into safe, light conversation to cover Stephen's nervousness about the impending offensive. He needed to talk, but Aiden wasn't sure it was to him. He drained his tea and faked a yawn. "I'm going to try and get some sleep. Goodnight."

"Goodnight, Foster... Aiden." Hawthorne inclined his head towards Aiden. "No heroics tomorrow. We've got our instructions. Take the mill beyond Mouquet Farm and the German second line."

"No heroics," repeated Stephen. His voice shook. "Goodnight, Aiden. Thank you."

"Goodnight, sir. Stephen." Aiden walked quickly away from them. By the time he settled himself down to sleep, his thoughts were already miles away. Each time he went into battle, he couldn't help but think of Jochen. What would happen if he found himself facing a Jerry on the field and it was Jochen? He'd be expected to kill him without a second thought.

Jochen was supposed to be the enemy. Not a friend.

If they met again... if they met tomorrow, Aiden would have to kill him.

Unless Jochen killed him first.

Morning came too soon. When Aiden was roused by the orderly officer an hour before dawn, he felt as though he'd barely slept. He was still yawning as he fixed his bayonet and climbed the fire step to guard against enemy fire.

To all intents and purposes, it looked like an ordinary start to his day. He guessed that was one of the reasons they were all behaving like it was. They'd lose the advantage of surprise if the Jerries expected what was coming—although he'd heard stories they already did. A couple of shots were fired at the enemy trench, men letting off fire to relieve the building tension. It didn't do much good. Tension ran higher than usual today.

How many of them would still be alive that evening?

That thought was running through everyone's mind, whether they admitted it or not. Of that Aiden was certain.

"Stand down, men." Hawthorne gave the order, and Aiden stepped down the couple of feet into the trench proper. He always felt too exposed on the fire step.

His stomach was rumbling by the time he'd finished cleaning his rifle, and it was time for breakfast. The meal was eaten in silence. He heard Hawthorne and one of the other officers speaking quietly but couldn't make out what they were saying.

"Is the offensive still going ahead, sir?" he asked Hawthorne as he passed by.

"Yes." Hawthorne's expression was grim. "It's still going

ahead." He didn't say anything else, but instead made his way to the trench periscope. "No morning duties today," he announced a few moments later. "Prepare yourself. We go over the top in twenty minutes."

Men busied themselves getting ready. Even Stephen was quiet, and he usually cracked a few jokes when they were readying themselves for an offensive. This one was important. Aiden had heard it could turn the tide of the war. They'd be home by Christmas.

He snorted. They'd said that his first year at the front. Home by Christmas.

Sergeant Burrows inspected the men. Hawthorne had returned to the periscope, keeping an eye on the enemy. Aiden tried not to fidget. He knew they were waiting for the right time, that it wasn't only their unit going over the top. Several mines had also been set to detonate as part of the offensive.

Hawthorne tightened his grip on his Webley pistol. He checked the time, whistle already in his mouth, ready to give the signal.

Aiden looked for Stephen and gave him a thin smile. Stephen was watching Hawthorne, his knuckles white where he gripped his rifle.

After what seemed forever, Hawthorne blew his whistle, and they surged over the top of the trench as one. Men clambered up the scaling ladders, formed a front line, and started the move forward.

Chaos ruled. Men dropped to the ground around him, cut down by German machine-gun fire. It wasn't the enemies' men who were dying but their own. A hare ran in front of him, its eyes bulging in fear.

Aiden ducked down, finding a shell hole. He peered over the top of it, returning fire. He'd lost track of the men directly on either side of him. Lifeless bodies hit the mud. Aiden felt in his haversack for the bombs he carried. What was the point? He was too far away for them to do any good.

The noise around him was deafening. He put his hands over his ears, but it didn't help. A body landed next to him. It was Burrows, or what was left of him. His eyes stared sightlessly ahead. Aiden felt for Burrows's arm. He yanked, trying to pull the body to a safe place, although the man was already dead.

Another body fell into the hole, this time landing on top of Aiden, burying him. He scrambled to get free. He couldn't breathe. All he could smell was mud. And death.

"He's dead. They're all dead," he whispered hoarsely.

The ground shifted under him, sending him flying. He lifted his head, tried to crawl back to the shell hole. They were outnumbered and outgunned. This wasn't victory—it was slaughter.

Aiden gritted his teeth. He was digging himself further into the mud. He reached for his rifle and gripped it tightly, then pulled himself to his feet.

He thought he heard a low moan nearby. Damn it. He couldn't see anyone. But he couldn't leave an injured man out here to die. He'd drag both of them back to the trench. Back to safety. No point in going forward. Not anymore.

Pain screamed through him. He jerked. Felt himself fall. His lower leg was on fire. God, it hurt. Aiden let off a couple of shots. Forced himself to stand again.

Another bullet. This time in his thigh. More pain. His left leg buckled. He fell to his knees. God, it hurt. It hurt so much. "I'm sorry," he screamed. "I can't. It…. I can't."

The darkness reached for him, a welcome refuge. He closed his eyes and surrendered to it.

~

Jochen couldn't believe it. After four years of fighting, this damn war was finally over. Or it would be in half an hour. At eleven on the eleventh day of November 1918.

Meanwhile he still had to survive the next thirty minutes. Whoever it was taking shots at them was determined to see this thing through to its bitter end. Jochen didn't see the point. The Armistice had been agreed upon and signed over five hours ago. Why couldn't they just lay down their weapons now?

He sat with his back against one of the supporting beams of the barn his unit was holed up in and reloaded his weapon. From his position he had a clear view of outside, but he was hidden from the enemy.

Enemy. He snorted at the word. They were all soldiers fighting this war. Men who had the misfortune to be on opposite sides. After that Christmas nearly four years ago, Jochen hadn't believed much of the propaganda about the Tommies. While it was true that not all men were decent human beings, most of them were, and Aiden most certainly was.

Was? Jochen swallowed. He didn't want to think of Aiden in past tense, as that would imply he hadn't survived this madness.

His fingers went to the identity disc around his neck and the button hanging with it. The gift Aiden had given him that Christmas. Jochen had wanted to keep it close but hidden, so it seemed the logical place for it, and the safest. He couldn't risk being caught with it, especially as the crown on it gave it away for what it was—a button from the uniform of a British soldier.

Despite himself, Jochen smiled. The button, and the

memories it evoked, had brought him this far, a reminder that beauty still existed despite the horror and waste of war. If he closed his eyes, he could still hear Aiden's song. Aiden had the voice of an angel, and the transformation in him when he'd sung had been nothing less than amazing.

Don't die on the wire.

Jochen had thought he'd seen it all when he'd spoken those words to Aiden. Although it was still not a way he'd want to die, he'd seen so much death since then his nightmares had started to merge together, snatches of reality, glimpses of horror that left him shaking when he finally woke. He found it impossible at times to separate what he'd seen from what he'd heard about and hoped he never would see. Men dying of gas—eyes streaming, coughing, trying desperately to catch their breath. Others had thought they'd escaped the weapon, but the effects had caught up with them later.

Men blown to pieces. Hands clinging to the wire all that was left of an unfortunate soul. Jochen could still hear screaming when he tried to sleep. He'd lost so many friends, and there were so many others, like Aiden, whose fates were unknown.

Arndt had perished at the Somme, his body found buried in the mud, his hands still curled around his gun. He'd been shot at close range. Grünberg had been shipped off to the Eastern Front in early 1915, a promotion it was rumoured, but Jochen had seen enough to know better. Weeks after the frowned-upon fraternization, their unit had been split up. Their superiors hadn't been happy when they'd heard about it, especially when some of their troops began protesting about orders to shoot men they'd come to consider friends. Soldiers were supposed to kill without question. The truce had given faces to their enemy, made them human.

Such thoughts were dangerous and would not be allowed to happen again.

"They're seeing this through to the end, aren't they?" Benedikt Auttenberg's question jerked Jochen back to the present.

He glanced up to see his friend and comrade giving him a bemused look. "That's what I'm thinking," Jochen said. "And before you ask, yes, I was contemplating the war."

"Again." Benedikt shoved some stale bread into Jochen's hand. "I swear it's going to be the death of you, my friend." He was ten years older than Jochen, a gentle man who, under different circumstances, wouldn't have hurt a fly.

"I've survived this long." Jochen munched on the bread. His stomach rumbled. He couldn't remember the last time he'd felt full. Food was getting harder to come by, and they ate what they could forage when they could find it. He'd heard stories that it wasn't much better back home. The German people were starving, and for what? They'd lost the war, and no one he spoke to had even wanted to fight in the first place.

"Luck," Benedikt said. "Given all the good men who have died around us, I figure that's all that has kept both of us alive this long." He ran one finger over the metal of his gun. "Do you think you'll go back to your studies once this is all over? Do you still want to teach?"

"I'm thinking about it," Jochen admitted. "My father was in poor health the last time I saw him. I don't want to go home only to leave him again. He's never been the same since my mother died."

"I can understand that." Benedikt smiled sadly. "I miss

my wife. She is my other half, and without her I feel a part of me is missing. How long were your parents together?"

"Thirty years." Jochen had often wondered what it would be like to find someone he felt so strongly about that he'd want to spend the rest of his life with them. He'd envied what his parents had and knew it was what he wanted, but he'd never met a woman he'd been attracted to in that way. "It was love at first sight, my father says."

Benedikt chuckled. "With us it was the opposite. We grew up together, and it took years before I realised that I was in love with her, that it was more than just friendship. She tells me she nearly despaired of me coming to my senses, but she waited until I did, as she didn't want to lose my friendship by scaring me off. Jutta." His voice softened when he spoke her name. "I can't wait to see her again. And our children. We have two boys. They've had too many years already without a father."

"You should be able to see them again soon."

"I hope so." A shadow fell over Benedikt's face. He ran a hand through his blond hair. "I haven't had word from them in a while. I fear...." His voice dropped to a whisper. "I fear that I might be going home to nothing, that this influenza epidemic might have already taken them from me."

It wasn't just civilians who had fallen prey to this new enemy. Strong men, soldiers, had also died from it. They'd gone from healthy, to sick with fever and coughing, to death in mere days.

Jochen shivered. Illness was an enemy none of them were equipped to fight. He'd heard rumours that the outbreaks were finally lessening. "All we can do is hope and pray they are still waiting for you. I worry about my father too."

He handed Benedikt back some of the bread, and they ate in silence for a few minutes. It was quiet outside. Eerily so. Others of their unit were scattered throughout the area; some had taken shelter in the farmhouse. Their orders were to stay alert, to defend their so-called stronghold from the enemy until the war officially ended.

"The first battle I fought was in this place," Benedikt said. "I've been posted in many different places, but here I am back in Belgium—in Mons—once more. Many think of that battle over four years ago as a great victory. All I remember is being surrounded by death." He shrugged. "It's ironic, isn't it? I suppose everything comes full circle, and there is no way of predicting how a tide will turn."

"One thing this war has taught me is not to presume anything."

"It's a minute before eleven." Benedikt peered outside. "I suspect those snipers, whoever they are, want this over as much as we do." He stood. "Do you have any idea who is out there exactly?"

"Does it matter? The war is almost over. We've lost." Although Jochen would never voice the sentiment, he was more than ready to give up fighting and return home.

"I'm not sure anyone actually wins a war. The other side has lost many men too. Life is never going to be the same for any of us." Benedikt laid down his weapon and walked towards the barn door.

"Benedikt!" Jochen hissed. "What are you doing? Have you lost your senses?"

"It's over, Jochen. I figure, let them have this place. We're leaving anyway." Benedikt kept walking. He opened the door. "The Armistice is now in effect. We're no longer at war. Why would they shoot me?"

"We should wait for Messner." Oberleutnant Messner was their commanding officer.

But it was already too late. Shots rang out. Benedikt jerked once. Twice. Then fell forward.

"No!" Jochen yelled. Without thinking he ran forward to help his friend. "The war's over! It's over. We've surrendered. You've won. You've. Already. Won."

"What? No. That's not possible." Despite his words, the soldier who had fired the shots suddenly sounded unsure. He started to stand from his hiding place behind a nearby abandoned cart but was quickly yanked back down again. "This is a trick."

Jochen cradled Benedikt in his arms. "It's all right. We'll get a medic." Tears rolled down Jochen's face. He'd seen so much death, but he'd never cried for anyone before. Why was he doing it now?

He heard someone running behind him. Messner kneeled down in the dirt with them. Others of their unit formed a circle around them, guns drawn. "Stay with him, Weber. I'm going to talk to their commander." He raised his voice. "I have no weapon. This war is over. Can we talk?"

Benedikt's voice was little more than a whisper. He clutched Jochen's shirt, pulling him closer. "I've had it." He fumbled around his neck for his identity disc. "Promise me something, Jochen. Take these to Jutta. Tell her I love her."

"You can tell her yourself." Jochen knew the words he spoke were empty. Benedikt was dying. Jochen had seen enough of it to know.

"Promise me." Benedikt gasped.

"I promise." Jochen kept holding him even when Benedikt's eyes slipped close and his head lolled back. He lowered his friend's body onto the ground. Jochen's hands were covered in blood.

He glanced up. Messner walked back towards him, another man—wearing the uniform of their enemy—at his side. Jochen hadn't seen where they'd come from. He didn't care. "I'm sorry, Weber," Messner said. "They didn't know. The news about the Armistice has only just reached them now."

"He didn't need to die." Jochen felt numb. He stood and rubbed his hands against his trousers. The blood wouldn't come off. Why wouldn't it come off? "The war is over. It's over."

"Yes," Messner said softly. "It's finally over."

CHAPTER THREE

"Aiden! Your breakfast is getting cold!"

Aiden jerked awake with a start. He hadn't realised he'd drifted off to sleep again, fully dressed and lying on the bed. He'd only intended to close his eyes for a few minutes in an attempt to rid himself of the grogginess that came from yet another night of not enough sleep.

"I'll be there soon, Mrs Hamilton," he said, although she wouldn't be able to hear him. There was no point in trying to yell back. He didn't do that anymore. Couldn't do that anymore.

He swung his legs off the bed, ignoring the twinge from his bad leg. Mostly it didn't bother him now, apart from the slight limp, but it didn't like the cold mornings. Neither did he. He reached for his pullover, yanked it over his head, and then ran his fingers through his hair in lieu of a comb. While he did possess one, he was in the habit of using his fingers, and habits were difficult to break.

A blighty wound, they'd called it. It meant he was one of the lucky ones. He'd get to go home, or so Thompson had told him when he'd visited Aiden in the hospital. Aiden didn't feel lucky. He'd taken two bullets in his leg, and infection had set in, not surprising with the couple of hours he'd spent lying in the mud before he was found. When he'd regained consciousness, he'd tried to crawl back to the trench but had been too tired and drowning in an ocean of pain.

But that wasn't the worst of it. He'd kept his leg, despite concerns he wouldn't, but his survival had come with a harsh price. His voice, his music—barely anything was left of it. The doctors kept telling him it would come back, that there was no physical reason why he could now only speak in barely more than a whisper. A few weeks in hospital, followed by time at home, and he'd be good as new.

Aiden snorted at the memory. He'd been to several doctors since, on the insistence of his parents, but they'd all told the same story. Nothing was wrong with him. Shame about the leg keeping him from returning to the front, but at least he'd survived while a lot of the lads hadn't.

It didn't feel like survival. Some days it was little more than a living nightmare.

"Aiden!" Mrs Hamilton would be knocking on his door soon at this rate.

"Coming!" Aiden wasn't sure why he still tried to reply like he wished he could. Sometimes, when he was feeling particularly optimistic, he hoped his voice would suddenly return, magically restored in some kind of miracle, as though it had never been gone.

He glanced over at the cane propped against the wall in the corner. *His* cane, although he hadn't used it in months. At the end of a long day, he often missed its support, but it was another reminder of everything he'd lost, of what he was no longer capable.

One day he'd get rid of it, but he was not ready to do

that just yet. To be honest, he wasn't sure he ever would be. Even so, he couldn't help but give it one last look as he left his bedroom and limped down the stairs to the kitchen.

"Good morning, Mrs Hamilton," he said as he sat down opposite her. She'd already served his breakfast. He ate the same thing every morning and sat in the same chair. Routine was good. More than that, it was safe, another lifeline to cling to when the bad memories returned to haunt him.

"Are you feeling poorly this morning?" Mrs Hamilton studied him from across the table. "Should you be going in to work at the theatre today?"

"I'm fine, Mrs Hamilton. Really. But thanks for asking." Aiden ate his porridge slowly and then poured himself a second cup of tea. "We have a new show starting this week. They need me."

He'd returned to his beloved Avery Theatre when he was well enough to do so. Once the star of their shows, he was now their handyman, doing whatever needed doing behind the scenes. He suspected they'd taken pity on him, which was why they'd given him the job, but he'd taken it without a second thought. Although he couldn't be a part of the music, being near it helped to calm him. He was still jumpy around loud noises. It didn't take much for his mind to take him back to that last battle. The memories of men falling around him, of the stench of mud and death—he wondered if he'd ever be truly free of it.

He'd fought in battles before the one at the Somme—the first Battle of the Somme they called it now—but his last experience in France as a soldier was the one he couldn't rid himself of.

"Your parents would be proud of you, Aiden," Mrs Hamilton said softly. She was an old friend of his mother's and had offered him a home when his parents had died two years ago from the influenza epidemic.

God, had they really been gone two years? He'd been back in Britain four years now. It felt like a lifetime ago, his life before the war a dream. He wished he'd never had to wake from it.

He fingered the cord around his neck, as he often did when thinking about the past. Although he no longer wore the identity disc of a soldier, he'd kept the cord it used to hang from and the button Jochen had given him. Meeting Jochen had been one of the few moments of the war Aiden didn't want to forget, although it was doubtful they'd ever meet again.

Even if Jochen had survived, why would he want to? Aiden had nothing to offer anymore. Without his music, he was no one. He couldn't step into that role again. He could only be himself.

"They always were," Aiden said. His parents had been horrified when they'd learned what had happened to their son. Molly Foster had told him they'd always be there for him. It had been an empty promise, but she'd made it with every intention of keeping it. Harold Foster had added his belief that Aiden would get through this, he was a strong person, and it was important for him to remind himself of that.

Aiden's father had reiterated that conviction right up to the day he'd died.

Mrs Hamilton smiled. "I still believe they're looking down on you, Aiden. They were good people, and so are you."

"Thank you." Aiden had tried arguing that, while his parents were, he wasn't really. He'd killed people, looked Jerries in the eye on more than one battlefield and still pulled the trigger. It wasn't a conversation he'd ever win, so he'd learned to just thank her politely and change the subject.

He drained his tea and placed his cup and saucer neatly on the plate he'd used for his toast.

"Don't you worry about those dishes, now," Mrs Hamilton said, like she did every morning. "I'll take care of them. You just worry about getting yourself to work. I'll see you this evening?"

"Of course." Aiden had nowhere else to go. They'd play their regular game of draughts, and then Mrs Hamilton would retire to bed. "I'm going to the library on my way home, but I won't be late for tea. Promise."

"I'll have it ready when you get home." Mrs Hamilton looked thoughtful. "Leave your other pullover on your chair in the parlour before you go. I noticed the elbow needs mending again. I'll do it for you today."

"You're too good to me, Mrs Hamilton." Aiden gave her a light kiss on the top of her head as he left the table. She might be his landlady, but she'd always been more to him than that. Sometimes he swore she mothered him more than his own had.

This had to be the place. Jochen studied the map he held and compared it to the hastily scribbled directions he'd been given at the Lily Tea Room. At least the girl there had been friendly. Most people he'd tried to talk to had smiled at him until he'd begun speaking and they'd realised he was German.

Two years after the war had ended and emotions still ran high. He couldn't blame them. People at home in

Germany were not feeling particularly friendly towards their former enemies either, especially with the state of the German economy. Instead of a victorious outcome, the war had left the German people worse off and faced with debts that were difficult, if not impossible, to pay. Inflation was ridiculously high, and many people were starving. Jochen had been luckier than most because his family had been well off. Even so, there wasn't much of their wealth left by the time his father had passed away the year before.

He'd been surprised to get a letter from a law firm based in London a couple of months ago. His father had never mentioned his aunt—Jochen's great-aunt—Wilhelmina. Apparently she'd been disowned by her family for marrying an Englishman. Jochen's father had been the only one who hadn't deserted her, but they'd lost contact after she left Germany and it had taken her lawyers a while to track him down. By the time they had, he'd died, and the inheritance left to him by his childless aunt was now rightfully Jochen's.

A few more letters between lawyers had resulted in Jochen now in the last place he'd figured he'd ever be. London.

"This has to be it." This time he spoke his thoughts aloud.

A sign over the theatre proclaimed it to be the Avery. Jochen's hands felt clammy. He wiped them on his trousers. His heart was thumping. He ran one hand through his hair after catching sight of himself in a window. It would have to do.

He fingered the button he still wore around his neck. Did Aiden remember him? Had he even survived the war? Perhaps this really was a foolish dream. But Jochen still had to try. Even if he was chasing a ghost, at least this way he'd find out for certain.

If nothing else, he wanted to say thank you. The memory of their conversation and Aiden's singing had helped Jochen through not only the war, but what he'd had to deal with afterward.

He hoped it wasn't a grave he'd be speaking to.

The front door was unlocked, although there didn't seem to be many people around. Jochen heard a piano, the same phrase of music repeated several times. A man was in the foyer leaning on a broom, an older man by the look of him, grey hair cut short above his collar.

"Excuse me," Jochen said, softly at first, before repeating his greeting louder when it appeared to be ignored.

The man finally turned around. His clothes were worn, mended several times, but clean and tidy. He had smile lines around his mouth, but he eyed Jochen with suspicion. "Can I help you, young man?"

"I hope so." Jochen saw the man's initial wariness grow. *Oh wonderful. Another lover of Germans.* He mentally sighed but continued anyway. He needed to do this, to hell with what anyone else thought. If Aiden told him to go away, that would be different, but until he heard the sentiment from Aiden, Jochen would see this through. "I'm looking for a friend."

"A friend?" The man gave Jochen a look of total disbelief. "I don't think anyone here would be a friend of yours. Try somewhere else."

"His name is Aiden Foster." Jochen tried again. "We met during the war. I...." Disbelief turned to outright hostility. Oh, what was the use? "He told me he performed here. I just wanted to give him a message."

"I can't help you." The man shook his head. "Go back to

where you came from. We don't want your kind here." He turned his back.

Can't help or won't?

As much as Jochen wanted to voice his thoughts, there was no point. He tried to peer past the man, to see if he could see anyone else in the theatre. The piano had grown silent, to be replaced by the sound of voices. Jochen strained to hear, but all he could make out was that whoever was speaking was female.

"If you see him, could you tell him I was asking after him?" Jochen took a deep breath. "Can I at least look around the theatre?"

"No. Only those who work at the theatre are allowed past here. Come back and buy your ticket for the show like everyone else." The words were spoken to the wall as the man didn't bother to turn around to answer.

"I might just do that. Thank you for your help." Jochen stomped out of the theatre and let the door slam behind him. He regretted the action as soon as he'd done it. If Aiden *was* there, behaving like that wasn't going to get Jochen any further in trying to see him.

It took a couple of blocks before Jochen's temper subsided. He found himself in front of the Lily Tea Room before he realised where his brisk walk had taken him. What the hell was wrong with the old man? All Jochen had wanted was to find Aiden, speak with him for five minutes, and leave.

Wasn't it?

The bell over the door of the tea room jangled, and the welcome aroma of tea brewing and warm scones temporarily distracted him. He'd been treated decently there. He felt too cold standing around outside and didn't feel like returning to his hotel just yet.

Another few minutes and he was sitting at one of the tables by the window. The girl he'd spoken to earlier brought him a pot of tea, a plate with two scones on it, and glass bowls holding generous quantities of butter and jam. "There you are, sir," she said.

"Thank you," Jochen answered politely, almost absently. She had dark hair like Aiden, and her accent was similar to his. While he had dark brown eyes, though, hers were green.

"Penny for them," she said, smoothing down her starched white apron.

"Excuse me?"

"You seem troubled. I noticed it the last time you were in too. Pardon me for not minding my own business, but my gran always says that sometimes you have to ask a man what's troubling him. And you seem like you could do with talking to someone."

Jochen stared at her in surprise. "You don't know me, and I don't know you." He picked up his cup. His hand trembled and the tea sloshed over the top and splattered across the tablecloth.

"Oh goodness. Let me wipe that for you." The girl returned a moment later with a thick napkin and used it to blot up the rest of the tea.

"Thank you." Jochen hesitated, then continued. "Are you sure you want to listen?" He allowed his growing frustration to enter into his voice. "Especially to a *German*?"

"People are still people. It doesn't matter where they're born and what side of a war they fought on." The girl smiled. "Let me get rid of this napkin and I'll let Uncle Vic know I'm having some tea." She leaned in. "He's good to me and lets me stop for a cup of tea when I need it as long as we're not too busy. A lot wouldn't, you know."

Jochen had just decided talking to her would be a mistake when she returned and sat down opposite him with her cup of tea. She seemed genuinely concerned, so he couldn't bring himself to be rude and tell her he'd changed his mind. He'd talk to her but be careful what he said.

"Your attitude isn't shared by a lot of people," he said, taking a sip of his milky tea. He added a spoonful of sugar.

"It's their problem if they want to be rude." She shrugged and then held out her hand. "Where are my manners? I'm Emily."

"Jochen." He shook her hand, not offering his last name, as she hadn't told him hers. It made it easier that way. He could talk to her and then walk out of the tea room and never see her again.

"It's nice to meet you, Jochen." Emily sipped her tea. "I'm not in the habit of talking to strange men, just so you don't get the idea I'm one of *those* sorts of girls. Because I'm not."

"Do you talk to all your customers?"

She giggled. "Of course not. But as I said, there was something about you that made me think I should, and I'm usually a good judge of character. Besides, my uncle is behind the counter and watching us. If you say or do anything inappropriate, he'll hunt you down and kill you."

"Charming," muttered Jochen. He held up his hands in mock surrender. "Don't worry, I wouldn't dream of being anything less than polite." He'd been brought up to respect women.

"Did you manage to find the Avery?" Emily asked. "I hope my directions were clear enough?"

"Yes, I found it." Jochen spread butter and jam on one of the scones before cutting it into quarters. "For all the good it did me." Perhaps she'd heard of Aiden? "I'm looking for a friend. A British man I met briefly during the war. He mentioned the theatre, so I figured I'd look him up while I was in London."

"Does he go there regularly?" Emily creased her brow in thought. "Perhaps if he does, you could go to a performance and see if you can spot him?"

"He was one of the performers. A singer. Perhaps you've heard of him? His name is Aiden Foster."

Emily shook her head. "Sorry, but I'm not a theatregoer." She looked apologetic before she added, "Do you know if he survived the war? I'm sorry to have to ask, but so many didn't. I lost my cousin over there. I still miss him."

"No, I don't. I'm sorry for your loss. I didn't lose any family in the war, but I lost too many friends." Jochen picked up one of the pieces of scone and ate it slowly.

He'd kept his promise to Benedikt and given his identity disc to his wife, Jutta. It had taken him a while to find her and the children. They'd survived the epidemic, but after news had reached her of her husband's death, she'd decided to move to the countryside to live with her parents. They owned a farm, and it meant her children would be surrounded by family. Her parents were in their sixties so could do with the extra help too.

Jutta had been grateful for something of her husband's, and pleased to meet someone who had been with him when he'd died. Jochen had told her what happened but left out some of the details, stressing the fact Benedikt had spoken of her and wished he could see her again. She'd smiled at that through her tears and asked him to stay on for a while.

As much as he was tempted to spend some time away from the city, he'd had to return to Berlin as his father's health was not good. He'd not fallen victim to the influenza but looked pale and weak compared to when Jochen had seen him last. It was a shock. And then, a year after Jochen's return home, his father was dead, and he was alone.

"What will you do now, if you can't find him?" Emily's question jolted Jochen back to the present.

"I'm not sure. I still have business to attend to in London before I return to Germany."

His great-aunt had not only left him a sizable fortune but also a cottage in the country. Jochen had dreamed of it the night before—or at least how he envisioned it might look, as he hadn't seen it yet. He couldn't imagine living there alone.

He fingered the button around his neck again.

His father had told him to find a wife and settle down, to find his soul mate rather than live alone. But as much as Jochen tried to visualise a future with a wife and children—he couldn't.

"Perhaps you'll find him before you leave." Emily drained the rest of her tea. "I need to return to work." She stood. "It's been nice meeting you, Jochen. I hope you didn't mind my company too much."

"Not at all." Jochen stood, seating himself again once she'd left. The conversation had helped him to make sense of his thoughts. After he settled his affairs here, he'd leave. There was nothing for him here. He had his studies and an offer of a teaching position in Berlin. Maybe it would be better to just go back to Germany, after all.

CHAPTER FOUR

"Is something the matter, Jack?" Aiden noticed Old Jack, as the theatre people referred to him, had been watching him more than usual. Jack tended to be fiercely protective of his "family," more so since the war had ended.

"Nothing important," Jack mumbled, turning back to his broom. He swept the same bit of clean floor several times, back and forth, each time with more force than the last.

"Look at me and tell me that." Aiden placed a gentle hand on Jack's shoulder. "You're not ill, are you? Is there anything I can do to help?"

Jack had a tendency to play things close to his chest when something was wrong. He'd treated Aiden no differently since he'd returned from the front, something Aiden appreciated. Knowing he wasn't the same man he'd been was difficult enough without reminders from others.

"No, I'm not ill." Jack stopped sweeping, leaned on his broom, and shook his head in what appeared to be disgust. "Some bloke was asking after you yesterday." He spat into his handkerchief. "A German." Jack spoke the word as though he'd tasted something foul. "Don't worry. I didn't tell him anything."

"A German?" Aiden's heart started to race.

"He said he knew you." Jack gave him a peculiar look. "Lying through his teeth, of course. You fought in the trenches. Only German you're going to know is a dead one." Jack raised an eyebrow. "Why do you want to know about him? No good will come of it. You know that as well as I do."

"They weren't all bad," Aiden mumbled. It wasn't a subject he wanted to broach with Jack, not now. Maybe later, if.... No, it was foolish. It couldn't be.... "What did he look like, Jack?"

"I didn't take much notice." Jack shrugged. "Didn't see the point. Young'un, like you, I guess."

"Please. It could be important."

"Fair hair. Couldn't tell you much else." Jack's expression narrowed. "What do you want me to tell him if he comes back?"

He'd told Jochen about the theatre. He'd know to look for Aiden here.

Was it Jochen, though? The description fit, but then it probably would a good number of Londoners too, although they wouldn't speak with a German accent. Jochen's friend, the one kicking the soccer ball around that day so many years ago in no man's land, had also been blond. It could be him, but why would Jochen have told his friend about the theatre?

Besides, why would Jochen be in London? Even if he'd survived the war, he would have gone back to Germany.

"I...."

Tell him he's wasting his time. I have nothing to offer him. Not anymore.

Aiden's hands were clammy. The words he wanted to speak died on his lips. "Ask him his name," he said finally.

"And?" Jack prompted. "You think you do know this bloke, don't you?"

Aiden nodded. "I might, but that doesn't mean I want to talk to him." He couldn't talk to Jochen, not sounding like this. But at least this way he'd know his friend was still alive.

"All right. Whatever you want, you just let me know. I'll make sure he doesn't bother you."

"Thank you." Aiden turned on his heel and walked away before Jack could reply. He wasn't ready for this. He never would be.

He had nothing to offer. Not anymore.

Jochen was enthralled. He hadn't expected to be pulled into the performance so quickly, but now he was, he didn't want it to end.

The band had begun to play again, a solo violin carrying the main melody line of the introduction. After a few moments, one of the men stepped forward and began to sing of oak and apple trees in a place called Linden Lea.

The words made Jochen glance up in surprise, as he remembered the verse Aiden had quoted six years ago. That had mentioned an oak too. Hope briefly surged through him, only to be followed quickly by disappointment. The singer had dark hair like Aiden, but his voice was different, huskier than Aiden's beautiful tenor. He was also heavier built. Aiden was slim. Jochen closed his eyes, calling up the image in his memory of the shy smile Aiden had given him.

He wasn't sure why he'd decided to come to the theatre. Perhaps he'd hoped to spot Aiden on the stage, to hear him sing one last time. Jochen was curious, he had to admit. It was easier to picture Aiden on stage after hearing him sing, but he wanted a context for it. This was Aiden's stage. He'd stood on these boards. Surely there still had to be something left of him here, if anywhere?

The tone of the music shifted as it moved into a new song. A woman was singing now. Her voice had a pleasant lilt to it. "Oh, Danny Boy, the pipes, the pipes are calling."

Jochen let his mind drift. Here among all these people, he felt a part of something again, something he hadn't really felt since the end of the war. They didn't know him, but that didn't matter. They were all here for a common purpose, to enjoy the performance.

He caught something out of the corner of his eye. A glimpse of dark hair, of someone moving at the corner of the stage. Jochen sat upright, straining to see.

No, it wasn't Aiden.

This was ridiculous. He hadn't come here just to find Aiden. He'd wanted to enjoy the show, to be a part of Aiden's world just for a while before he had to return to the reality of his own.

"But when ye come, and all the flowers are dying. If I am dead, as dead I well may be, ye'll come and find the place where I am lying, and kneel and say an Ave there for me."

Jochen felt tears prick at his eyes. He wiped them quickly before anyone could notice. The woman kept singing. Jochen closed his eyes, seeing the grave in his mind she was singing about. It had Aiden's name on it.

He stood quickly and stumbled from the theatre, ignoring the glares and the hissing to be quiet. Once in the foyer, he leaned against the wall, his breathing coming in gasps. The image had hit him quickly, and he hadn't expected it. Had he been looking in the wrong place for Aiden? What if he was lying in some grave, just like the song, sleeping in peace waiting for someone to come for him?

Jochen bit his lip. He wiped his brow with his handkerchief and then shoved it back into his pocket. He'd only known Aiden a few hours, but years later he still couldn't get the man out of his head. Not just his head, but his heart....

It had been a mistake coming here. He'd been haunted by this for far too long. Aiden was a memory who had helped Jochen through a terrible time. His life was looking up now. He had a future he should pursue, and he needed to lay his ghosts to rest.

But he didn't want to just remember Aiden through his music. He owed him more than that. It wasn't just Aiden's music that had drawn Jochen to him and kept him in his thoughts, but Aiden himself. Jochen had felt something between them before he'd heard Aiden sing, a connection that might have had the potential to grow to at least a friendship if they hadn't been fighting on opposite sides.

He'd sat up late the night before composing a note, rewriting it several times before deciding it would have to do. He'd kept it in his pocket, just in case, although he hadn't been entirely certain why he'd written it. If he saw Aiden, he'd talk to him directly. If not....

Just because Jochen felt that way didn't mean Aiden did. He'd been lonely, in a strange land, fighting friends who, while good men, didn't understand him in the way Aiden seemed to within just a few short sentences. Was that what this was about? He'd found someone who he thought understood him, so he'd desperately tried to read something more into it?

Jochen sighed. That pretty much described where he was right now. Desperate. He'd lost his family and had kept to himself since returning to Germany. He had no friends, not bothering to make the effort to go much further than his books. He was popular at the university and had plenty of acquaintances, and people he met up with regularly, but he wouldn't lose any sleep if he never saw them again.

His father had always said if you meet your soul mate, you know. Was that what he was looking for now? Who he was looking for?

Because that was hardly sensible, not to mention dangerous and illegal.

Jochen was getting foolish ideas about an Englishman who might not be interested in pursuing a friendship, let alone anything more, and that was even if he was still alive.

Not getting. Got. He'd had them since they'd met, but with everything else going on, he'd shoved it mostly to one side until now. He couldn't afford the distraction while he was trying to stay alive at the front, and then his focus had been looking after his father. Jochen's future had seemed clear-cut at the time. Finish his studies and try to get a teaching job. He'd needed an income, had to think about his future.

Aunt Wilhelmina had changed that. Now he was in London, and for the first time since his father's death, he didn't have to worry about the future, at least not financially. Dreams were safe when there was no chance of them ever coming to fruition.

"No, I haven't. Don't worry about it, lad."

A familiar voice caught Jochen's attention. The old man he'd spoken to the day before was talking to another man, tall, slender, and with dark hair.

"Aiden?" Jochen whispered, too softly to be heard.

From the back it looked just like him. A thud behind Jochen made him jump. He glanced around in a sudden panic, for a moment back in the war, reaching for a weapon he no longer carried and hadn't in years. But it was only a woman dumping a pile of heavy books on a nearby table.

Jochen turned back to the old man, but whoever he'd been talking to was gone. *Damn it!* Jochen strode over to him. He couldn't go on like this. He needed some kind of resolution one way or another in order to walk away from the situation and truly put it behind him.

"Hello again," Jochen said.

"Hello." The old man eyed him up and down. "I didn't expect to see you here again. What do you want?"

Jochen counted to five before replying, making the effort to keep his tone calm and nonconfrontational. "I saw you speaking to someone before." He took a deep breath. "I know you probably don't want to tell me who it is, and you won't believe me when I tell you he looked like the person I was asking you about yesterday."

"You're right about that. I don't want to tell you who it is." The old man looked more curious than anything, and not quite as aggressive as the last time they'd spoken. "You're a persistent one, I'll give you that. Get to the point, though. I'm not getting any younger."

"Could you give him something from me?" Jochen fished the note out of his pocket. He'd sealed it inside an envelope with Aiden's name on the front. He handed it to the old man. "It's important he gets it as soon as possible."

The man nodded. He looked at the envelope and then back at Jochen. "I'm not saying he's here, but what will you do if he doesn't reply to your note?"

"I'll walk away and leave him alone. You won't see me again."

"I'll see he gets your note, then." The old man slipped it into his pocket. "Just mind you keep to that, though. I'll not have you upsetting anyone for no good reason."

So it had been Aiden. At least that was what the old man seemed to be implying. "I promise." Jochen wasn't about to meet with Aiden if he didn't want to. Sometimes the past was just that, and it was where it needed to stay. At least this way he'd know for sure. "Can you tell me something, though? It was him, wasn't it? He's still alive?"

The old man studied Jochen for a long moment. "Yes, it was, and he is." He turned to go and then turned back as though he'd forgotten something. "What's your name? He'll want to know who the note is from."

In case he didn't want to open it?

Aiden was alive. He'd survived. That was all that mattered, wasn't it? But why wasn't he on stage? Why wasn't he still doing what he loved? The answers Jochen had needed so badly only brought more questions.

"My name is Jochen," he said. "Jochen Weber." A lump formed in his throat. He shoved his hands into his pockets and walked away. He had nothing else to say.

Except to Aiden, and he might not want to listen.

All Jochen could do now was wait and hope he did. But whatever the outcome, he'd promised to walk away, and however difficult, that was what he intended to do.

The theatre had a different feel to it once the show was over. While the magic didn't completely disappear, it seemed to go into a form of hibernation, resting until needed again. Rehearsals had a different feel to them than a performance, although Aiden enjoyed watching the outline of a show start to become reality.

With the stage empty, and the performers in their dressing rooms removing their makeup and costumes, the theatre was quiet. These were the moments Aiden dared to snatch back a little of his past. He stood on the stage, closed his eyes, and remembered what it felt like to stand up here and sing.

God, how he missed it. It felt as though a part of him had been ripped away along with the music he could no longer create. Perhaps it had only meant to be a fleeting gift? He'd done nothing wrong, nothing that would justify losing it.

Was it just hibernating, like the theatre between shows? If so, he was tired of this never-ending winter.

A song replayed through his mind, the final one from the show tonight. It was one he loved, about roses, love, and dreams. A smile tugged at his lips. Without thinking he opened his mouth and began to sing.

But all that came out was a whisper, a horrific reminder of everything he'd lost.

What was the point? His voice was never coming back. He was tired of this reality. He had nowhere to retreat from it, nowhere to hide. Not from this and not from the nightmares he was haunted by.

He'd survived the war, but sometimes he wondered why.

"Aiden?"

Aiden shrugged himself out of his thoughts. They weren't a path he should be following. Self-pity wasn't about to do him any good, yet despite his best intentions not to wallow, it seemed to find him when he least suspected it would.

"Hello, Jack." Aiden forced a smile. "I'm about done here." He'd packed most of the props away, apart from what was needed for the first act for the next performance on Thursday. Tomorrow was his day off. There were no performances on Wednesdays.

"You need to stop torturing yourself, lad." Jack shook his head. How long had he been standing there? "You do a lot of good around here, even without your singing. Don't forget that."

"If you say so." Aiden kept his tone light, almost joking. If not for Jack, Aiden would have climbed into that dark abyss long ago and not bothered to come out.

"Do you remember that German bloke I told you about?"

"Yes?" Aiden swallowed. "Did... did he come back?"

"That he did." Jack pulled an envelope from his pocket. "He left this for you. He said I was to give it to you as soon as I could, so that's what I'm doing."

"Did you ask his name?" Aiden's heart was thumping. If Jochen had been in the theatre again, why hadn't Aiden seen him? Jochen had managed to speak with Jack twice. Was he avoiding Aiden? Or maybe it wasn't Jochen and this was a letter saying what had happened to him?

"That I did." Jack glanced between the letter and Aiden. "But I'm guessing you already know what it is."

"Jochen," Aiden said quietly. "It was Jochen."

"That it was, or so he said." Jack handed Aiden the letter. "He asked after you, but I didn't tell him anything. I figured that was up to you. But he did say if you didn't want anything to do with him, you wouldn't hear from him again. He won't be round here again."

Aiden's hand shook as he read his name on the envelope He'd never seen Jochen's handwriting before. Didn't know whether to believe this was real or not. His other hand went to the button around his neck. Did Jochen still have the button Aiden had given him? "He's still alive. Jochen's still alive."

"I figure if you want to see this friend of yours, it's your last chance, so I wouldn't stare at that for too long." Jack cleared his throat. "I'll be going now. Good friends are difficult to find, and given your reaction, my guess is you consider him one. If I've got that right and you do, at least let him know that."

"I will." Aiden ripped open the envelope and scanned the words quickly, his mind only partially on what Jack had said. "What do you—"

But Jack was already gone.

Aiden reread the letter. His mouth was dry. His lips formed the words as he reread again, more slowly this time, savouring them.

Dear Aiden,

You probably don't remember me. We met briefly in 1914 during an unexpected truce between our two countries, and had a thought-provoking discussion about literature. You shared a few stanzas from Tennyson with me.

I'm in London on business and hope to see you again. I had worried you might not have survived the war, and it gladdens me to know you did.

If you would consider meeting with me, I will be at the Lily Tea Room until it closes today. I have included directions at the end of my letter. If you do not come to the tea room, I will presume you do not want to pursue this further. If so, my apologies in dredging up the past, but I wish you well.

> *Kind regards,*
> *Jochen Weber.*

The letter was definitely from Jochen.

He didn't need the directions to the Lily Tea Room, as he knew where it was. He'd gone there several times. It was a quiet place and friendly, and they made a decent cup of tea. One of the waitresses had tried to talk to him but given up after Aiden pointedly refused to engage her in small talk. He'd been polite but no more. He had nothing to talk about, nothing he wanted to discuss. Only experiences she wouldn't have understood, and he wanted so badly to forget.

Aiden ran his fingers over the letter once more before sliding it back into its envelope. What now? Jochen would only be at the tea room for another hour or so. Had he changed? Had he been injured in the war? Aiden wished he'd asked Jack for more information, but it would have only served to draw attention to how badly Aiden needed to know. Jack had already guessed Jochen was a friend. Aiden hadn't referred to anyone as a friend in a very long time.

Was that really what he and Jochen were? Friends? They'd only met so briefly, and not really been given the chance to see if they could have been. Yet it felt as though Jochen had been a part of Aiden's life for so long. A memory, a presence just out of reach. Sometimes Aiden woke from a particularly bad nightmare, sure he'd heard Jochen's voice....

He didn't want to think about how close he'd come to giving up.

His meeting with Jochen was one of the reasons Aiden had returned to the theatre. To his music. To hang on to something good in a life that felt at times as though it was falling apart.

Could he risk trading the memories of Jochen for a reality that didn't mesh with what Aiden remembered of the man? It had been so long ago, and too much had happened. Sometimes Aiden wondered if he'd embellished their meeting and added things that hadn't taken place. Like Jochen's smile and the way his eyes lit up when he laughed.

Or maybe this was exactly what he needed to do to put this behind him and move forward? He'd wondered sometimes if clinging on to this bit of his past was preventing him from leaving the war behind.

Aiden walked slowly to the small room at the back of the theatre where he kept his tools. He retrieved his coat from the hook behind the door, folded the envelope carefully in half, and put it in his pocket. He kept a cane at the theatre too, just in case, but he wouldn't need it today any more than he needed the one at home. The theatre was only a couple of blocks from the tea room. It wouldn't take long to get there. He didn't have to go in. All he had to do was see Jochen, to see if he'd changed. He hoped not. Aiden knew he wasn't the same man he'd been when they'd met. He wouldn't wish his experiences on anyone. Someone he'd known had to have come through this war unscathed, to be living a life that felt more than just survival.

But how would he know for sure without speaking with Jochen?

The wind ripped through him, cold fingers sending shivers down his spine. He pulled his coat tightly around him and began walking briskly. Darkness came early this time of year, and although it was still a few hours away, Aiden always felt it before it arrived. His leg twinged, but he ignored it.

It didn't take long before he found himself across the road from the tea room. He hesitated, trying to decide whether to go in. All he needed was a glimpse of Jochen to satisfy himself it really was him.

Aiden crossed the road. He could see someone sitting at the table by the window, but he wasn't close enough to make out details. He took a couple of steps closer, only a few feet away now.

He let out the breath he was holding. The person by the window was a woman so hadn't been Jochen, after all. But that didn't mean he wasn't there. Other tables gave a good view of the street but were harder to see from outside. What if Jochen was sitting at one of those?

Standing outside was no good. He was going to have to go inside. All he'd need was a minute, and he could walk straight back out again. Jochen hadn't seen him in six years. He might not even recognize him, and then Aiden could just slip away.

But was that fair to Jochen? Especially as he'd gone to the trouble to write the letter and give it to Jack. Aiden knew what Jack was like and that his attitude tended to scare off people. Surely it said something that Jochen had been prepared to return and try again?

Or was Aiden just being fanciful and foolish?

He wished he knew.

There was only one way *to* know. He pushed open the door and walked inside. The bell jingled as he entered, and he froze. Damn it. He'd forgotten about the bell.

He scanned the tea room quickly. At a table in the corner, a man looked up with a start. He had a book in his hand. He'd been reading.

He had blond hair, a darker shade than Aiden remembered. He wore a dark blue pullover. It brought out the colour of his eyes.

His gaze fixed on Aiden. His expression was difficult to read.

Coming here was a mistake. Seeing Jochen again was too real, too raw. Aiden took a step backwards and felt his bad leg buckle. He grabbed at the counter, frantically trying to hide it.

"Aiden." Jochen mouthed Aiden's name, but the word had no sound. He dropped his book and pushed back his chair. "Aiden? Is that really you?"

CHAPTER FIVE

"Aiden?" Jochen repeated Aiden's name, suddenly unsure.

The man in front of him looked like Aiden, but something about him didn't seem right, given what Jochen remembered.

Jochen strode across to him quickly, ready to help. Aiden shook his head, although he still hung on to the counter. "Jochen," he whispered. "It's good to see you again. Give me a minute, will you?"

"I can help if you need it. Are you... hurt?" Jochen looked around for a cane that might have fallen to the floor but couldn't see one. Was Aiden sick? Was that why he sounded like that?

"No, and I don't need any help." Aiden stared at him as though he'd seen a ghost. "Go sit down."

Jochen signalled Emily. "Could you bring some more tea, please?" If Aiden didn't want to stay, that was fine, but Jochen wanted to be prepared for the possibility he might. He pulled out the other chair, in case Aiden wanted it, and sat back down at the table. The book he'd been reading was still open. He closed it and pushed it to one side. He hadn't been taking in much of it anyway. Instead he'd glanced outside every few minutes, in the hope Aiden might still appear.

After a few minutes, Aiden seemed to regain his composure. He limped over to the table and sat down. "Sorry about that," he said, his voice still that strange hoarse whisper. "Bad leg. It gives out on me when I least expect it."

"Don't worry about it." Jochen kept his tone light. What the hell had happened? It wasn't just his voice and his leg; he could see lines around Aiden's eyes he was sure hadn't been there six years ago. "It's good to see you. I wasn't sure you'd come."

"I almost didn't." Aiden bent his head. "I... didn't.... A lot has happened. I wasn't sure you'd still want...." He lifted his head and looked Jochen up and down. "You look well. Old Jack gave me your letter. He said you'd come looking for me yesterday too. I'm surprised you remembered the name of the theatre."

"I haven't forgotten anything about our conversation," Jochen said. He pulled the cord around his neck out from under his shirt so the button was resting against his pullover. "I kept this too."

Aiden smiled at that. He mimicked Jochen's action. "I kept yours too." He bit his lip. "So much has happened, Jochen. I'm not that person anymore."

"I'm not the person I was six years ago either, Aiden." Jochen leaned across the table and briefly placed one hand over Aiden's. "I don't think anyone who fought in that terrible war could be."

He wanted so badly to ask what had happened, but he couldn't. This had to be Aiden's story to tell. Perhaps if he told Aiden something of his own experiences it might encourage him to talk.

Aiden glanced at the book Jochen had been reading. His eyes widened. "It's Tennyson!"

"*Idylls of the King.*" Jochen had searched the bookshops in London until he'd found one. "I wanted to find out what happened next."

"You might find it helpful to read about what happened before as well." Aiden chuckled. He seemed to relax as their conversation shifted onto familiar ground. "Most things make a lot more sense in context."

"In life as well as literature?"

"Here's your tea, sir." Emily placed a fresh pot of tea on their table, a small jug of milk, and two clean cups and saucers. "I'll take the other pot and your used cup. It will be cold by now."

"Yes, it is," Jochen said. "Thank you." He'd poured one cup but had only taken a few sips from it.

Emily didn't seem to be able to take her eyes off Aiden. "I didn't realise you were the friend Jochen was looking for." Her tone had shifted to a mix of surprise and disbelief.

"You've been here before?" Jochen asked Aiden.

"A few times."

"He's been coming in since we opened last year," Emily said. "Does this mean I'm finally going to get a proper intro-duction?"

"I don't know," Aiden said. "Does it?"

Emily sighed. "I see we've still got a way to go before the season of Christmas miracles." She grinned. "But at least now I know your name, so I figure that's a good start, right?"

"I suppose so." Aiden looked resigned. "You're presuming miracles still exist. They don't."

"Enjoy your tea, gentlemen. We close in forty-five minutes. Don't let it get cold now." Emily seemed more amused by his response than anything else. She picked up the almost untouched pot of tea and Jochen's used cup and saucer before walking away.

"So... you and Emily know each other?" Jochen asked.

"No, despite her best efforts to ply me with small talk every time I come in here." Aiden poured milk into his cup, then the tea, and stirred it slowly.

"She's probably just trying to be friendly." Jochen thought Aiden had been almost rude to the girl.

"Probably." Aiden shrugged. "I'm not one for talking much these days."

"Would you prefer we didn't?"

"No!" Aiden looked up. "I didn't mean that. I'm enjoying... this reminds me of the conversation we had years ago." He sighed. "As I told you, Jochen, I'm not the man you met back then. Too much has happened."

"Not just to you, my friend." Jochen realised he'd called Aiden "my friend" as soon as the words left his mouth, but Aiden didn't seem to notice or be bothered by it. "Have you ever talked to anyone about it?"

"Have you?" Aiden placed his spoon on his saucer. His expression softened. "I'm sorry, that was rude of me. I'm so used to... being defensive... I suppose, that I don't...." He flushed. "I don't know why, but you're easy to talk to. You were then too. And I'm making an idiot of myself. Sorry."

"You've nothing to be sorry for." Jochen waited for Aiden to continue, but he didn't. "To answer your question, no I haven't talked to anyone. I tried once, but it was a waste of time. You had to be there to understand what we went through, and most who were don't want to talk about it. It's me who should be apologising. Expecting you to just talk about your experiences during the war was insensitive, even rude."

"Who did you try to talk to about it?"

"My father." Jochen still remembered the conversation all too well. "He wanted to know, but ten minutes later he didn't." His father's expression had twisted into pain and fear. "I think what I told him gave him more of an idea of what I've been through, and it scared him. He lost my mother before the war. He was never the same afterwards."

"I'm sorry." Aiden hesitated. "Did he come to London with you? Your letter said you were here on business?"

"My father died a year ago. He'd been in poor health for some time. The doctors said it was a heart attack." Jochen had gone in to the university to organise something for a lecture. When he'd arrived home, his father was dead. He'd missed being with him by minutes.

"I'm sorry," Aiden said again. He picked up the spoon and studied its surface. "I lost both my parents in the influenza epidemic two years ago. I keep telling myself that at least I had time with them after I got home. If I hadn't been discharged in '16, I wouldn't have had that."

"It doesn't make it any easier," Jochen said softly. "Discharged because of your leg?"

"Yes. I took a couple of bullets in it during the first Battle of the Somme. Nearly lost the damn thing because of infection. It's mostly all right now but doesn't like the cold weather." Aiden ran his finger along the side of the spoon. "It does have a tendency to give out when I least expect it, though, even now. Not sure why."

"Perhaps you're more tired than you think?" Jochen suggested. Now that Aiden was talking, Jochen was determined to encourage him to keep doing so. His voice was still a whisper, but it wasn't quite as hoarse as it had been.

"Perhaps. I used a cane until the war was over. Partly because I needed it, but also because it stopped the whispers about why someone my age wasn't doing his duty and fighting on the front." Aiden snorted. "A lot of people still believe it's some romantic quest, like slaying a dragon and saving the kingdom. I was lucky. At least my injury was an obvious one. I've seen chaps home on leave and out of uniform given white feathers because people think they must be cowards. Cowards? They have no bloody idea of what went on over there. None at all!"

Jochen decided he wasn't going to comment on the analogy, especially as he suspected from the British perspective his role was that of the dragon.

"A friend died in my arms a few minutes after the Armistice," he said. "It was so pointless." Jochen's hand shook. He placed his other hand on top of it to still it. "Sometimes... sometimes when people try to be sympathetic, it just makes it worse. I know they mean well, but I want to scream at them that they weren't there. That they couldn't know."

Aiden nodded slowly. "I've found it's easier not to talk about it at all. I don't want their sympathy or to see it reflected in their eyes. Often the sympathy is the worst thing to deal with. I've no tolerance for platitudes anymore, or much of anything else. I keep telling myself they mean well, but it doesn't change what happened. It doesn't bring anyone back." He put his cup to his lips but placed it back on its saucer without taking a sip. "I lost a good friend in that last battle. His name was Stephen. At least they found his body. It's horrible for his family getting the news but better than not knowing. Some of the others from our company are still missing. They never found one of our commanding officers. Decent chap, about our age too."

"Benedikt was older, had a wife and family. I found them after the war and told her about his last moments."

Jochen still had nightmares about Benedikt's death and wished he hadn't had to talk about it.

"I'm so sorry, Jochen." Aiden looked suddenly embarrassed. "You must think me terrible talking about what happened and bringing everything up again for you like this. I didn't mean to. It's just... I haven't talked about this for so long. Not since the hospital. I... I didn't think." Embarrassment turned to horror. "Oh God, you would have lost friends in the battles I fought in. I hope I wasn't the one who killed them."

"Please, stop apologising." Jochen poured some tea and took a sip from his cup. It gave him something to do while he collected his thoughts. Aiden was right. Jochen had lost a friend in that first Battle of the Somme: Arndt, who had been there with them during the Christmas truce. "I haven't talked about the war in a long time either." He shrugged away the chill that went through him. "If you killed some of my friends, I probably killed some of yours."

"Listen to us. We're talking about killing each other's friends while we're drinking tea, as though it isn't—wasn't—real." Aiden's expression darkened. He glanced around as though worried he might be overheard. "I have nightmares about the men I killed. I can still see them when I close my eyes."

"So do I." Jochen hadn't tried to speak to anyone else about his experiences after seeing his father's reaction. He hadn't attempted to talk to his father about it again either. He hadn't wanted to see that expression on his father's face again, especially as he'd already begun to suspect their time together was limited at best. "It's strange, isn't it? We haven't spoken in six years, and yet in a way it's like that Christmas was just yesterday. I'm talking to you about things I don't speak about with anyone, except this time it's...."

"Not about literature?" Aiden nodded in agreement. "Mrs Hamilton says some friendships are like that. People see each other again and pick up where they left off like the time in between never happened."

"Mrs Hamilton?" asked Jochen. Aiden had used the word friendship. Did he think of what they had as a friendship? Jochen hoped so. He really hoped so.

I'd like it to be more.

He dismissed the thought. It couldn't be, and he was being foolish even thinking it. He supposed he'd carried the memory of Aiden for so long now that he'd built it up to be something else. Being with Aiden like this again, it was a good feeling, right somehow. Despite all the horrors they'd both been through, it had remained constant. A friendship they'd both said they hoped could have been.

Maybe now it would be.

"My landlady. Although I'm sure she sees herself as more of a foster mother. I keep reminding her I'll be thirty in another four years, but it doesn't dissuade her in the slightest." Aiden chuckled, but it was forced. "*She* keeps telling me what I need is to find a good woman, settle down, and start a family."

"Is it?" Jochen felt a coldness grip him inside. The thought of Aiden doing that... it wasn't something Jochen wanted to think about. "Is that what you want, I mean?"

"A family?" Aiden seemed surprised Jochen had asked. "No, not really. It doesn't seem fair to expect anyone to put up with me. Damaged goods and all that. Besides, I'd have to find a woman I'd want to be with, and that hasn't happened either. I figure things happen if they are meant to, and if they're not, then they don't. My mother used to tell me that all the time, but then she thought...." Aiden looked away and grew silent.

"She thought what?" Jochen asked.

"Nothing." Aiden cleared his throat and then took a long drink of tea. "So," he said brightly, "you said you were in London on business?"

"You're changing the subject."

"Yes, I am." Aiden gave him a glare. "So?" He stirred his tea again, although there was no reason for it.

"All right." Jochen wasn't about to get into an argument about it. Their conversation so far had felt very natural, but there were still things Aiden obviously didn't want to, or couldn't, talk about. Was his mother's comment something to do with his voice?

"It's not something I want to talk about." Aiden's voice had that hoarseness back. Jochen struggled not to flinch at the sound of it. It reminded him of gravel, stones being dragged across a once-smooth surface, disfiguring it so its original form was no longer recognizable.

"All right," Jochen said again. What the hell had happened to Aiden? "I won't ask, then." Saying he was sorry didn't quite seem the right thing to say. It wasn't appropriate, and they'd both used the phrase so often already in this conversation that it also didn't seem enough. "I'd like to keep in touch if that's all right with you." Jochen studied Aiden, not sure whether he'd overstepped a line, considering how little they really knew each other. "If it's not and you want to just walk away when we've finished our tea, I'll respect that, as I told your friend at the theatre."

"I don't want you to walk away. Some... things are too raw to talk about. I'm not sure I'll ever be able to talk about them. I'm sure you have topics you feel that way about too." Aiden appeared to consider for a moment. "Why don't we agree to let each other change the subject abruptly when we need to and not to call each other on it?" He held out his hand. "We could shake on it?"

"All right." Jochen shook Aiden's hand. He had a strong grip, and his palm was warm against Jochen's skin. Jochen let go reluctantly after an acceptable time. "I apparently also need to find another response that isn't 'all right.' You'll be tiring of it soon."

"It's fine." Aiden's mouth twitched up into a grin, his humour returning now they'd agreed on a course of action. He really was a handsome man, especially when his eyes twinkled like they did now, an echo of what he'd been like when he'd sung that Christmas. "All right, even."

Jochen laughed. "One of the reasons I'd like to stay in touch is that I don't know anyone else here. It's a relief to see a friendly face and someone who doesn't want to shoot me on sight because I'm German. I knew it wouldn't be easy, but I guess I really had no clue as to the degree of hostility there would be. Foolish really, considering how things are at home."

"The same, but in reverse?"

"Yes." Jochen knew he was extending the conversation past where it needed to go. He didn't want it to end, but it had to soon. He saw Emily watching them. She glanced at the grandfather clock sitting against the far wall. They didn't have long before the tea room closed. "You asked me about my business in London? Apparently I have—had—a great-aunt who married an Englishman. She left me an inheritance, part of which is a cottage outside London. I need to go see it tomorrow and decide what to do with it. It's in a village called Crayford, east of Bexleyheath. I don't suppose you have any idea where that is?"

"I know where it is." Aiden steepled his fingers, obviously thinking about something. When he spoke again, it was hesitantly. "I don't have to work tomorrow. I can come with you, if you'd like. We can take the train. Make a day of it."

"I'd like that." Jochen smiled. "Very much so. Thank you." He drained the rest of his tea, which had gone cold, like his previous cup. Apparently Aiden was just as much of a distraction when he was present as when he wasn't. "We should leave before we're thrown out. I think they want to close."

"I'm surprised they didn't throw us out five minutes ago. Your friend Emily is usually less subtle with her reminders." Aiden leaned in. "I suspect she likes you." He stood and tipped his hat at Emily.

"Where would you like to meet?" Jochen asked.

"It is very good to see you again, Jochen. Why don't we meet outside the Avery about ten tomorrow?"

As they left the tea room, Jochen held the door open for Aiden. "It was good to see you again too, Aiden," he said once they were outside. "The Avery at ten sounds perfect. I'll look forward to it." They shook hands, somewhat awkwardly. Aiden turned and walked slowly away. Jochen watched him until he turned a corner. He pulled his coat more closely around himself. He hadn't realised just how warm it was inside until Aiden had left. "It was *very* good to see you again."

CHAPTER SIX

"There's a hotel up ahead on the left," Aiden said. "Perhaps we could ask for directions?"

Jochen looked up from the piece of paper he held. "That's a good idea." He tucked it back into his pocket. "I'd like to make sure we're heading the right way before we go further."

The morning had been very enjoyable so far, for the most part. When Aiden reached the theatre, Jochen was already waiting. They arrived at the station with ten minutes to spare before the train left for Crayford, and Jochen had insisted he pay for both tickets, despite Aiden's protests. Aiden was giving up his day to help Jochen sort out part of his inheritance, so he figured any costs incurred would be part of the expenses associated in doing so.

They'd talked quite a bit on the train journey, although they were careful to keep their voices down. Jochen's English was very good, but his accent was unmistakably German, which got him a few glares and rude comments. He had winced at several of them but still replied with a cheery good morning to the first few. Unfortunately, a particularly disagreeable old man had joined their carriage a few stops later, someone Aiden doubted had even got as far as the front. Those were the worst, he'd decided. Full of opinions on matters they knew nothing about. Finally Aiden suggested he and Jochen move seats to the other end of the carriage so they wouldn't have to listen to it anymore. He should have done it sooner, as by then Jochen had already become quiet and withdrawn to the point where it took Aiden a few attempts to bring back the good-natured man he was beginning to get to know.

"Do you want me to ask?" Aiden asked. His leg was getting sore, but he wasn't about to admit that to Jochen. They'd already walked for about fifteen minutes from Crayford Station, and he wasn't used to it, at least not without his cane. It was cold today, too, and a fine mist hung in the air, although it hadn't rained as yet. He hoped they'd find this cottage and be able to take shelter before that happened.

"No, I can do it." Jochen frowned. "You're limping. Are you sure you're all right to walk further?"

"I always limp," Aiden told him. Damn it. He thought he'd hidden it better than that.

"More than usual, then." Jochen held the door open for Aiden when they reached the hotel.

Crayford looked much the same as Aiden remembered it. He'd come with his parents for a day out before he'd gone off to war. A pleasant memory for him to take with him, his mother had called it, a day away from the bustling city of London. Aiden preferred London now, although he hadn't then. It was easier to lose himself in a crowd. In London he was one of many returned soldiers, and no one talked about it. In a village like this, everyone knew each other's business, or made it a point of finding out if they didn't.

He vaguely recalled the hotel, although he'd only seen it

from the outside. His mother had packed a picnic, and the weather had been pleasant and warm. The village had struck him as slow, with a relaxed air about it. Six years later, its atmosphere hadn't changed. It was reassuring to know that it hadn't, that something hadn't been affected by the madness he'd lived through.

A fire was burning in the hearth inside, and the interior of the hotel had a homely, welcoming feel. A couple of easy chairs were by the fire, but Aiden only gave them a glance, despite the temptation to sit closer to the source of the heat. It was a relief to get inside, out of the cold, just for a few minutes. Jochen strode up to the bar and ordered two beers. There was a table close to the counter. Aiden found a chair and sat down. He wasn't about to turn down a pint, especially as it meant they could take a break before going further.

The man behind the bar eyed Jochen with some degree of suspicion, but his tone was still light and cheery. "I haven't seen you here before."

"That's because I haven't been here before," Jochen said, replying in the same tone. He retrieved the piece of paper from his pocket and smoothed it out with his hand. "I was hoping you could give me some directions. We're looking for Lavender Cottage."

"What will you be wanting with the cottage?" The man slammed the beer Jochen had ordered down in front of him.

A woman walked over to the counter from where she'd been wiping down tables. She had a tea towel over her shoulder. "I'm sure the young man has a good reason for asking, Roger," she said. "Don't you, dear?"

Aiden got to his feet and walked over to the bar. He wasn't about to let Jochen deal with any more aggravation today. He'd already made the mistake in waiting too long before suggesting they move seats on the train. "It's wonderfully warm in here," he said, taking a seat at the counter. "Have you had any luck in getting directions to the cottage yet, Jochen?"

As he expected, both Roger and the woman turned to look at him. The woman frowned, and then she smiled. "Can I get you some water, dear?"

"I'm fine." Aiden plastered on a smile, reached for his glass, and made a point of taking a long drink. While she probably meant well, it wasn't the first time he'd been offered water because of the way he sounded. If only it was that easy. "It's been a while since I've tasted a decent Guinness," he said. "That was certainly worth the walk from the station. Thank you."

"Mary—" Roger started to say, but she shushed him.

"So what will you be wanting with the cottage?" This time her question was directed at Jochen. "I'm afraid if you're looking for old Mrs Bracken, you're too late. She passed away earlier this year, poor thing."

Jochen frowned. "Poor thing? Was she ill?" He'd told Aiden the lawyers had said his great-aunt had died peacefully in her sleep.

"I'm not sure that's any of your busi—" Roger stopped abruptly when his wife shot him a glare.

"Now, how do you expect to find out what the lad wants if you keep asking him those sorts of questions," she said pleasantly. "You must excuse my husband. We don't get a lot of visitors around these parts, especially since the war." Mary looked a little younger than her husband, although there was some grey in her auburn hair. She had a kind smile.

"Mrs Bracken was my great-aunt," Jochen said. "She left me the cottage, so we've come to take a look at it." He held out his hand. "I'm sorry. I should have introduced myself. I'm Jochen Weber. This is my friend, Aiden Foster. I don't know many people here, so he was kind enough to offer to be my guide today."

"Aaah," said Mary, as though everything was now explained. "We had no clue she had a great-nephew. She never spoke of you." She shook his hand and then Aiden's, nudging her husband to do the same. "I'm Mary Grant, and this is my husband, Roger. Mrs Bracken never talked much about her family. I gathered they treated her poorly, probably didn't approve of her marrying her Jeremy. She mentioned a nephew, though, seemed fond of him. Now what was his name again?"

"Theodor?" Jochen prompted.

"Yes! That was it." Mary shook her head. "She was a good woman, well respected, and would do anything for anyone. She hated that our two countries were at war. You're her nephew, you say?"

"Great-nephew. Theodor was my father." Jochen sipped his beer. "He died last year. Great-aunt Wilhelmina's lawyers have been trying to find us." He'd told Aiden that apparently she'd written to his father, but the letters had been returned unopened with a scribbled note that he no longer lived there. Given the little he remembered of his father's family, he suspected they'd probably intercepted them. "He never mentioned her to me either. All of this has been somewhat of a surprise."

"Hmm." Mary looked Jochen up and down. "There is some resemblance between you and your great-aunt, I suppose. Something around the eyes. Isn't that right, Roger?"

Roger snorted. "You're always seeing someone in someone else. People look like themselves, not bits and pieces of their folk who have come before." He suddenly turned to Aiden. "What do *you* think, lad?"

"What?" The question took Aiden by surprise, and he spluttered into his glass. "I don't know," he said finally. "I've never really thought about it."

Roger seemed to take Aiden's answer as agreement. He shot his wife a triumphant look. "See, not everyone thinks as you do."

"If you say so, dear." Mary continued on as though he hadn't spoken. "So... Mr Weber, are you planning to stay awhile?"

"I haven't really decided," Jochen said.

Aiden glanced at him. Wasn't he planning to go back to Germany once his inheritance was settled?

"I have a few other things I need to work out first," Jochen continued. "Taking a look at the cottage is one of them. Is it in good repair?"

"Mrs Bracken took good care of everything. We've kept it tidy for her since her passing," Mary said. "That's what she would have wanted, after all. You're not planning on selling it, are you?"

"I don't know," Jochen said. "I can let you know either way if you'd like, as you were friends of my great-aunt's." He drained his beer. "Thank you for your hospitality. I truly appreciate it."

"Mrs Bracken would have been horrified at anything less, and yes, we would like to know your plans for cottage." Mary looked over at the door as it opened and two men entered. "You'll be wanting to get on now and take a good look around. If you have any more questions, please don't hesitate to come visit us again."

"I'd like to find out more about Great-aunt Wilhelmina," Jochen said. He nodded towards Aiden. "Do you want to sit for a while longer?"

"Give me a moment to finish my beer." Although Aiden hadn't spoken much, he'd taken his time drinking it. He finished the last of it, placed the empty glass on the counter, and stood. His leg protested a little but felt much better for the rest.

"Would you like to borrow an umbrella?" Mary asked. She gathered up their empty glasses. "It's another ten minutes' walk to the cottage, and it looks like rain."

"Thank you, but we'll be fine," Aiden said quickly. He didn't want the temptation of using it as a cane. It was only a short walk. He was out of practice. He could do this.

"If you insist, dear." Mary's expression reminded Aiden of Mrs Hamilton when she began one of her "but I'm only concerned" speeches. What was it with women trying to mother him?

"You'll be wanting those directions, then," Roger said. He shot Aiden a sympathetic look, but there was some amusement in it.

"Yes," Aiden said. They'd been here long enough, and he could feel Mary watching him and wondering what was wrong with him. Most people didn't ask, but she might, especially given the number of questions she'd subjected Jochen to. Aiden didn't want anyone's sympathy. It wasn't the worst part of all of this, but it came close. He especially didn't want to see it in Jochen.

"Please," added Jochen.

"You saw the bridge on your right when you came in here?" Roger asked. When they both nodded, he continued. "Once you're over that, and past the Cray River, continue up the road in front of you for about ten minutes. Lavender

Cottage is on your left. Can't miss it, the name of the place is on the front gate."

"Thank you." Jochen tipped his hat to Mary as they left. He waited for Aiden to catch up and then closed the hotel door behind them. "Perhaps I should go back and borrow that umbrella," he said, looking up at the sky.

"A bit of rain won't hurt." Aiden jammed his hat down further on his head and rebuttoned his coat. Once they started walking, the cold wouldn't be much of an issue either.

"I see villages are the same whatever country you're in." Jochen kept his pace relatively slow, more so than he'd done when they'd walked from the station.

"Full of people who know everything and want to know everything else?"

Jochen laughed. "I rather like that," he said. "They were kind, and I got the impression they meant well." His tone changed to something more wistful. "I wished I'd known more about Great-aunt Wilhelmina. It feels as though I'm intruding into something that shouldn't be mine by coming here."

"If your great-aunt left you the cottage, it's yours." Aiden stopped for a moment on the bridge, looking out at the river that ran beneath it. "I'm sorry about that man on the train and for all those people who have been rude to you."

"Why? It's not your fault." Jochen stood next to Aiden and rested his hands on the top of the wall running along-side the bridge. His breath formed small white clouds in the cold. Jochen's scarf had come loose from under his coat and was beginning to slide off from around his neck towards the ground. Without thinking, Aiden reached out and tucked it back in again. Jochen startled, but instead of protesting, he smiled. He had a beautiful smile, very gentle and warm. "Thank you. It's too cold to go fishing in the river for it."

"Huh? What?" Aiden realised he was staring at Jochen. "Oh right. Yes. It's definitely far too cold for that. We should keep walking. It's not the weather to be standing around in either." He hoped the cottage wasn't too cold, but at least it would be dry. Light drops of water landed on his hand. The rain that had been threatening to fall had finally made the decision to arrive.

"I can understand why people react to my accent," Jochen said as they walked. "I represent what they fought against, and I'm a reminder that their loved ones are never coming home."

"You didn't want to fight any more than I did." Aiden noticed trees growing on both banks of the river. The ones on the other side were tall, so had probably been there awhile. How much had they seen of this small village? How many generations had played under them or walked by them as he and Jochen were doing now? He shivered and shoved his hands into his pockets. This area had a sense of history to it, that was for sure, but also possessed a calmness he hadn't felt in years. It was the same feeling he used to get when he lost himself in his music. Listening to it still helped, but it wasn't the same as when he'd been able to perform it himself.

"No, I didn't, but I still did my duty, and that included killing to stay alive." Jochen shrugged. "I'm not sure I'll ever be able to justify that part of it, but then again maybe that's the point? Once we start justifying it, what next?"

"I don't know. I don't want to know." Aiden looked around. He'd sworn he'd heard a bird singing, but he couldn't see it anywhere. "Did you hear that?"

"Hear what?" Jochen slowed down again.

"I heard a bird singing." Aiden hoped he didn't sound as crazy as he thought. There was definitely nothing there. "I must have been mistaken."

"I saw a few in the trees when we were on the bridge. I have no clue what they were, though." Jochen glanced up at the sky. It was very dark, and the rain was falling faster. "They've probably decided to be sensible and take shelter before they drown. I think we should do the same. Can you walk any faster?"

"Yes." Aiden had been dawdling, and he knew it. Houses and smaller cottages were on either side of them now they'd crossed the river. Lavender Cottage shouldn't be too far away. He picked up his pace. Many of the cottages seemed to have fanciful names, and not all of them flowers. "Somerset, Twilight, Sanderson." He spoke them aloud as they walked past. "I wonder how they got named."

"A lot of these look as though they've been here for years," Jochen said. "So do the signs on them." He pointed to one. "That one looks older than the cottage it's for. I wonder if their present owners even know or whether the sign just came with the cottage when they bought it?"

"Or inherited it." Aiden stopped in front of the next one. It was a little smaller than those they'd just passed. He took a deep breath, the smell of lavender permeating his nostrils. The front garden was full of it, and there were bushes either side of the front door. A sign in decorative script on the front gate proclaimed it to be Lavender Cottage, but he would have known it for what it was even without the sign.

Despite being empty, the cottage had an inviting feel about it. Curtains hung from the windows, a pale green colour with shutters to match. Jochen opened the front gate, which squeaked as he did so, and held it open for Aiden. "Shall we?" he asked.

"After you." Aiden hung back. This was Jochen's past, and quite possibly his future if he decided to stay. Aiden was simply a guide on this day. It didn't seem right to infringe on the excitement of this discovery, or even be a part of it.

"Thank you," Jochen said, but he still held the gate open after he walked through it and waited for Aiden to follow. Once he had, Jochen sprinted up the front path towards the door. "Come on. There's no point in standing out in the rain now we don't have to."

"I agree." Despite his hat and coat, Aiden was beginning to feel quite wet. He couldn't wait to be inside and out of the weather.

The sky lit up, and then a few minutes later there was an enormous clap of thunder. Aiden ducked instinctively and looked around for cover. He noticed Jochen did the same, although his friend seemed to recover his wits sooner.

Jochen fumbled in his pocket for a key and opened the door. "Welcome to Lavender Cottage," he said softly, although his voice wavered. Thankfully he didn't comment on either of their reactions to the thunder.

The inside of the cottage wasn't exactly what Aiden expected, although come to think of it, he hadn't really thought much about what it would be like. It was simply furnished, but he knew enough to know the pieces were expensive. The front door opened into a living room. Two comfortable-looking sofas were positioned on either side of the fire, and a rolltop writing desk stood in one corner. In the other was an upright piano.

Jochen walked over to the piano and lifted the lid. He turned to Aiden, a look of delight on his face as he pressed one key and then another. The tone was clear, rich, and perfectly in tune. "Isn't this wonderful?" he said.

"Do you play?" Aiden asked, torn between hope and fear that Jochen did. He frowned, memory catching up with him. "No. Wait. You told me you didn't."

"I didn't." Jochen played a scale very slowly. "I tried again after the war, this time on the piano instead of the violin. It suits me better, but I'm not that good. Still, I enjoy it, and as long as no one is around to hear the way I torture the instrument, I suspect there's no harm in it."

"Oh." As much as Aiden wanted to hear the instrument played, he knew he'd be tempted to try to sing along with the music, and he didn't want Jochen to hear it. Not that there was anything to hear, but, no... he couldn't take the chance. Sometimes a noise did come out, a horrible one that sounded like something being forced through a mincer.

On top of the piano were several photographs. One was of a woman about his age playing a violin, another of a man seated at a piano, this piano. Aiden peered closely at the photograph of the woman. There was something about her that was familiar.

Jochen followed Aiden's line of sight and leaned over to pick up the photograph. He turned it over and read the words on the back aloud. "Wilhelmina Bracken. 1885."

"Mrs Grant was right," Aiden said. "There's a family resemblance." She was a very attractive woman, and her smile reminded him of Jochen's. It was unusual to see a photograph taken that long ago in which someone was smiling. Most of what he'd seen had been very serious.

There was another photograph on the piano of the two together. They were standing outside the cottage, by the front door, holding hands.

"Jeremy Bracken," Jochen confirmed. Jeremy was taller

than his wife by a good six inches, and his hair was dark in contrast to Wilhelmina's, who was fair like Jochen. "They look about our age." He held the photograph for a few minutes, running one finger around the frame. "She left behind her family to be with him. She must have loved him very much. I wish it hadn't had to be that way. I would have liked to have met her."

"Do you think she did the right thing?" Aiden asked. From what Jochen had said, she'd given up everything to be with the man she loved.

"They look very happy together," Jochen said slowly, putting the photograph back where it belonged. He glanced at Aiden and then back at the photograph. "I think...." He cleared his throat. "I think that sometimes you have to follow your heart and to hell with it. Often there's only one chance at love, and what happens if you ignore it? I wouldn't want to be alone wondering what if."

"She must have been very sure that he loved her too." Aiden took off his hat and coat, hung them on the coat stand by the door, and then sat down heavily on one of the sofas. "Life isn't always that simple."

Jochen nodded slowly. "Some days I think it should be. My father always said my mother was his soul mate. I'd like to think Great-aunt Wilhelmina found hers in Jeremy."

"How long were they together? Do you know?" Aiden wondered if he'd ever find someone he wanted to spend the rest of his life with, someone for whom he'd risk everything just as Wilhelmina had done. She'd left her country and her family to be with Jeremy. He envied her bravery in doing so. It wasn't something he was sure he could do, even if his so-called soul mate did walk into his life.

"Nearly forty years. He died about six years before she did. Pneumonia, apparently. They never had children."

Jochen walked over to the other sofa, but he didn't sit on it. Instead, he stared into the cold, empty fireplace. "I can't imagine what that would be like. To find the love of your life and have to carry on without them." His voice dropped to a whisper. "My father knew. He told me the years he spent alone after my mother's death felt like another lifetime."

"He wasn't totally alone. He had you." Aiden wasn't sure what else to say, but he felt he needed to say something, to try to break the sombre mood into which Jochen was descending.

"Yes." Jochen looked up from the fireplace. "Do you want me to see if I can get this fire lit? It's not that much warmer inside than out."

"How long do you want to stay? We don't want to be too late back."

"Oh, that's true." Jochen looked disappointed at the reminder. "I'll go look around for a bit. Do you want to come with me, or would you prefer to stay here?"

"I'll stay here." Aiden hesitated before continuing. "Unless you want some company? I... I thought you'd prefer to be alone, given... I don't want to intrude."

"You wouldn't be." Jochen studied Aiden for a moment. "At least let me find a blanket if we're not going to light the fire. You look cold now you've taken your coat off."

"It was wet," Aiden explained. Not that his coat would dry where it was without a fire, but he'd wanted to be free of it. "I... I don't like being in wet clothing." He clenched his fists and then forced himself to unfurl them, to ignore the memories he associated with the feeling. It had been so damp in the trenches, but it was nothing compared to lying for hours in the wet, stinking mud. He'd been so sure he was going to die that day. So many had.

Aiden turned away. He closed his eyes. He didn't want Jochen to see him like this. The memories were only that. They were in the past.

Why did they insist on plaguing him, and why now? Why couldn't they just leave him alone?

"I'll find you a blanket," Jochen said softly. "Unless you want me to stay?"

Aiden shook his head. He opened his mouth, but no sound came out. Not even a hoarse whisper. He shook his head again, feeling himself flush.

God, he didn't want to know what Jochen must think of him. This was Jochen's day. He must be struggling with his own emotions with being in this place.

"It's fine, Aiden. Take your time. I won't be far away." Jochen placed a gentle hand on Aiden's shoulder but withdrew it quickly. "I understand. I have these moments too."

Aiden opened his eyes, but Jochen had already gone. He wanted to call to him, to tell him to come back. In that moment Jochen had touched him, that they'd been close, his memories had suddenly gone as quickly as they'd come. Aiden put his hand on his shoulder, still feeling Jochen's warmth there.

That settled it. He truly was losing his mind. A touch that brief would not leave any warmth. It was the memory of it he was feeling, nothing more. A snatch of memory that even now chased away the darkness that was never far away.

"Did you say something?" Jochen asked from behind Aiden.

Aiden turned to see Jochen poking his head from around the doorway. He walked out, a blanket in one hand, which he gave to Aiden. "Thank you," Aiden whispered.

Jochen smiled and walked back into the other room. The blanket he'd given Aiden was a quilt. A bed-sized quilt.

Had Jochen gone into the bedroom? Aiden felt his cheeks flame. He glanced in the direction Jochen had just gone and started to his feet. Images flooded his mind. Not the horror of the battlefield he'd just experienced, but something else.

Musings, not memories.

Jochen first thing in the morning, his hair tousled in sleep. The two of them in this cottage, drinking tea in front of a roaring fire. Aiden's hand on Jochen's knee, as they enjoyed each other's company and conversation.

Bloody hell!

What was he thinking? He shouldn't have thoughts like this. Mortified, Aiden let the quilt fall to the floor. He stumbled from the room, away from Jochen, needing to be as far away from his friend as possible.

The back door was locked from the inside, a heavy brass key in the lock. Aiden opened it and staggered outside. The cobbled path was slippery and wet. He felt his bad leg give out and cried out as he landed with a thump in the garden.

He struggled frantically to right himself but couldn't find traction in the mud. He heard himself cry out, felt himself.... *No! Please God, no.*

Strong arms enveloped him, helping him to his feet. "You're all right. It's fine, Aiden." Jochen sounded concerned. More than concerned. Scared. "Look at me. You're not in France. You're safe. I promise. You're safe."

He stared up into Jochen's face, into his bright blue eyes, and immediately looked away. As though the day could possibly get any worse. He pushed Jochen away. "I'm fine," he snapped. "Please... I'm...."

Aiden limped back into the house, frantically wiping at

the dirt on his trousers. It was only dirt. Not mud. And not much of it.

He couldn't remember the last time he'd so totally lost his grip on reality.

Jochen followed him back inside but kept his distance, something for which Aiden was grateful. He wasn't sure what had mortified him more, the fact Jochen had seen him like this, or how good it had felt having Jochen's arms around him.

France. Jochen had mentioned France.

"How did you know?" Aiden mumbled. He didn't turn around to look at Jochen, but he knew he was there. He could feel Jochen's presence. It screamed at him, couldn't let him forget what had just happened.

"That you were out there, or that you were back in the war?" Jochen's voice was strained. It was no wonder, considering.

"Back in the war." Aiden didn't see the point in denying it. He'd never denied it.

"Because I've been there." Jochen moved closer after he spoke. "I came home after the war, as you did, but it followed me, just as I think it's followed you."

"I'm sorry." Aiden shivered. Jochen put a hand out to steady him. Aiden backed away. He couldn't let Jochen get that close again. He couldn't risk Jochen seeing his reaction. He didn't trust his reaction. God, he wanted to be held like that again.

Knowing he did scared him.

"Don't be." Jochen smiled, that same gentle smile, but there was sadness in it this time. "Please. Don't be. As I told you, I have these moments too." He guided Aiden back to the sofa. "I'm going to light a fire. We can catch the later train back, but neither of us are going out in that weather until it eases."

"But...." Despite the kind words, Aiden didn't want to believe Jochen suffered from these waking nightmares too. He wouldn't wish it on anyone.

"You're cold and wet and so am I." Jochen's tone was still polite but firm. "Stay there, Aiden. I'll be back in a moment."

Aiden nodded. "I'm sorry," he whispered. This couldn't happen again. Any of it.

"I know." Jochen walked out of the room but stopped at the doorway to glance at Aiden again. He murmured something Aiden couldn't quite hear, but he could have sworn the words Jochen spoke were, "So am I."

CHAPTER SEVEN

"Get off me!" Aiden couldn't breathe, couldn't think. Buried by the rapidly cooling corpse he was trapped beneath, all he could smell was death.

He fought to free himself, desperately, like a man possessed. One last heave and the body rolled over, off Aiden, and he crawled out, pressing himself against the side of the shell hole. A few deep breaths and he dared to glance at what was left of the man who'd trapped him.

Aiden blinked. He rubbed at his eyes. The man's uniform was German, not British. No, that wasn't right. Cautiously Aiden edged back. Sightless eyes stared back at him. Accusing. Empty. Blue eyes that had once smiled at him.

Jochen.

Aiden screamed.

And woke to find himself tangled in the blankets of his bed at home. His throat was dry, sore, and he was sweating, dripping with perspiration. His heart was beating fast. He felt cold. Numb. Terrified.

Aiden heard a knock at the door. He jumped.

"Are you all right, dear?" Mrs Hamilton called through the closed door.

"Yes," Aiden called in his usual hoarse whisper. The word tasted like sandpaper, his voice croakier than usual.

"If you're sure now?" Mrs Hamilton sounded worried.

"Yes." Aiden licked his lips, trying to get some moisture into his mouth. "Thank you," he managed to add.

It took him a few minutes to realise she'd gone. He breathed a sigh of relief. Outside, the moon was high in the sky, the light through the gap in the curtains bathing the room in a gentle glow.

Only a nightmare, just a bad dream. It wasn't real. Was it?

Aiden yanked the blankets back over him. He shivered, reached for the glass of water on his bedside cabinet, and took a long drink.

He hadn't had a nightmare like that in a while. And he'd never dreamed of Jochen, at least not like that. Dreams of his friend had always been a welcome change from the usual horror that plagued his sleep.

His thoughts went back to earlier that day, of how he'd felt when Jochen had been close. How much he'd wanted it, wanted more. Even now, after that nightmare, the memory of Jochen's touch calmed Aiden, sent a warm feeling through him, a smile to his lips. Glancing down, he was horrified to see a slight tenting in his pyjamas, the beginnings of an erection. Not much of one, but enough to confirm the cause of it.

He wanted Jochen, wanted to be with him. He found it more difficult to ignore his body's reaction, easier to push aside the emotions that went with it.

This nightmare hadn't started as such, but it had turned to one quickly, the scene changing after Jochen in his dream had reacted the way Aiden feared he would. He and Jochen had been back at the cottage, but the afternoon had taken a different direction than it had in reality. Aiden hadn't backed away, but had leaned into Jochen's touch, asked him to stay, and kissed him.

Jochen's eyes had widened, and he'd pushed Aiden away. What the hell was Aiden thinking? Jochen had offered friendship. Not this. Why would he want... this?

The question was a good one. Aiden wasn't sure why he wanted it either. What he felt for Jochen was wrong, wasn't it? Men weren't supposed to want other men. But despite being brought up a good Christian, Aiden knew he wasn't the only man who had desired another. Time spent in the army had opened his eyes. He'd seen things, seen men together. Men who were more than friends, although they hid it for the most part. They had to.

But Aiden wasn't like that. He liked girls. Didn't he?

He'd never met a girl he wanted to be with. And certainly not one he'd reacted to in the same way he had with Jochen. Jochen was the first person Aiden had allowed himself to get close to, emotionally, since he'd come home from the front. He wasn't even sure how it had happened. Jochen was easy to talk to. He understood what Aiden had been through, not just understood, but... no, it was more than that.

What did Jochen want from him? He was going back to Germany once he'd sorted out his inheritance. Aiden would never have to see him again.

It was better that way, wasn't it? Not only was this crazy, but dangerous and illegal. He didn't want to end up in prison, especially for admitting how he felt to a man who most likely didn't return those feelings.

Aiden had turned his back and walked away when they'd returned to London. He'd already made his decision.

Jochen had a future. He wanted to pursue his studies and to teach. Better to leave him to get on with his life.

It was better this way. For both of them.

Wasn't it?

"Do you want to sell the cottage, Mr Weber?"

"Yes." The question took Jochen by surprise, although it shouldn't have. "No." He'd decided that morning that he would. He had no reason to stay in Britain. Not anymore. Yet why couldn't he tell the man in front of him that? "I'm not sure. When do you need to know?"

Mr Harris peered at Jochen over gold-rimmed glasses. The lawyer was an elderly man but very sharp. Apparently he was an old friend of Jeremy Bracken's—Great-uncle Jeremy—which was why he'd been chosen by the couple to handle their affairs.

"Mrs Bracken left you the cottage, Mr Weber. It's yours to do with as you please. Therefore I really don't require an answer unless you require my help in organising the sale of it." He wrote something on the paper in front of him, then smiled at Jochen. "I understand all of this has been quite a shock for you, with you unaware of your great-aunt's existence until recently. All the rest of the paperwork is done. Why not keep the cottage in the meantime? It doesn't matter whether it is sold now or in six months' time. Whatever your decision, our firm will be here to help."

"Thank you. You've been very helpful."

Harris was right. Discovering a relative Jochen hadn't known existed had been rather a shock. It had also shed light on an aspect of his family he hadn't wanted to admit. They'd disowned Wilhelmina merely for loving a man they didn't approve of.

Perhaps it was part of the reason Theodor Weber had cut ties with them. Visits to the family estate had seemed strained in later years, more so as Jochen became older. He hadn't heard the content of the arguments that had gone on behind closed doors, but the last one, shortly after his mother died, had resulted in his father stalking out and never returning.

"Mr Bracken was a good friend to me for many years," Harris said. "He asked me to take care of his wife, and that includes ensuring that her final wishes are adhered to." He stood and held out his hand. "I mean what I say, Mr Weber. If you require our help with anything, please do not hesitate to contact us. Harris, Ludlam, and Wode is at your service."

Jochen stood and shook Harris's hand. "I will do that, thank you."

A few minutes later, he found himself standing on the street, briefcase tucked under his arm. People walked around him, some giving him a smile as they passed by, others clearly annoyed that he was in the way. A motor vehicle passed close by, and Jochen jumped back just in time to avoid being sprayed with water. Its driver waved cheerfully and continued on his way.

Would he have done so if Jochen had spoken?

Dealing with the lawyer had been a pleasant experience, despite the subject matter. He'd talked about Jochen's great-aunt and uncle at length and seemed genuinely pleased to meet Jochen. His clerk had been another matter. The man had been polite enough, but Jochen had seen his reaction when he'd heard Jochen's accent. It was a reaction he was quickly tiring of.

The war was over, but he doubted many Londoners would ever forgive him for it. As he'd told Aiden, he could understand the reaction, but he'd had enough of it. He wasn't personally responsible for the death of their loved ones—or at least he hoped he wasn't. He hadn't wanted to fight in the damn war, and he'd lost people he cared about too.

It had been several days since he and Aiden had visited Crayford together. Aiden had been very quiet on the train journey back to London, hardly saying a word. He'd merely nodded or shaken his head in reply to any conversation Jochen attempted. He'd also kept his distance, as though trying to squeeze into as much of the corner of the window seat as he could. The scenery had appeared to take most of his attention. He'd held himself stiffly, his jaw clenched, his eyes unfocused.

Was he still embarrassed because Jochen had seen him caught in a memory from the war? Jochen slipped his hand under his coat to the button he wore. Despite Aiden's turning his back when they'd said goodbye and not even offering a handshake, Jochen couldn't bring himself to take off the button. He'd associated it for so long with the only good thing to come out of the war. The memory of their meeting, and Aiden's singing, had given Jochen something for his sanity to cling to. He'd wondered so many times why he was still alive when so many weren't. He'd spoken the truth when he'd told Aiden he had moments when he too was caught in those nightmares of death and despair.

They'd become much worse after Jochen's father had died, and he'd felt so very alone. He'd been tempted on more than one occasion to contact his father's family, but each time something had stopped him. His father had good reason for severing ties with them. Jochen couldn't disrespect his father's memory by going against that.

When the thought of a long, lonely future had stretched ahead of him, he'd found himself returning to the button around his neck and the memories it evoked. While there was still something in the world as beautiful as Aiden's song, surely there was still hope?

The last few nights the nightmares had returned, although he hadn't been plagued by them in months. But they weren't just of the war, of having his friends—of Aiden —dying in his arms, but of a bleak future, alone and forgotten. He knew next to nothing of Great-aunt Wilhelmina. All that was left of her were photographs that told stories he wanted to know more about. She'd had friends in Crayford who spoke warmly of her, and a husband who had loved her, although she'd spent her last few years without him.

Jochen had pushed so many people away. He hadn't wanted to—couldn't—talk about the war, so it had been easier to keep to himself. And now, the one person he'd felt he could talk to, the one person he wanted... hoped... to spend time with had turned his back on him.

It had been a mistake finding Aiden. They'd slipped into easy conversation so quickly, and Jochen had enjoyed his company. When they'd been at the cottage, Jochen had allowed himself to daydream, to imagine what it might be like to live there. Not alone, but with Aiden, his earlier musings so much easier to visualize now he'd seen the cottage, and Aiden in it.

Better to have loved and lost, than never to have loved at all.

Jochen snorted and pushed the quote aside. That Englishman, Tennyson, had no clue what he was talking about. Besides, this wasn't love. How could it be? He was being ridiculous now. Just because he enjoyed Aiden's company didn't mean he loved him. Loving another man, and one who would never return those feelings? No, not just ridiculous, but mad. Despite not particularly looking forward to the idea of a future alone, Jochen liked the idea of several years in prison sentenced to hard labour even less.

If... and that was a big if, he found someone he truly loved, who felt the same way about him, wouldn't it be worth the risk?

But he hadn't, so there was no point in torturing himself with the idea. He'd built up the memory of Aiden in his mind for so long that he could no longer tell the difference between it and reality.

It wasn't just Aiden who was haunted by memories of the war.

So why then had Jochen offered comfort without thinking? Why had he wanted to brush Aiden's hair from his face and softly kiss his forehead?

Because he was an idiot, a desperate man who wanted so badly for all of it to be true. No, there was nothing for him here. Not anymore. Aiden clearly wasn't interested in a friendship. Jochen had tried to hide his reaction when Aiden had walked away, but that didn't make it hurt any the less. Even now, if Jochen allowed himself to dwell on it, it still did.

A familiar bell yanked him out of his thoughts. He looked up in surprise to find himself walking past the Lily Tea Room. Not only were his thoughts tormenting him with his memories, they were dragging him back here.

What harm could it do to go there one last time? At the very least, he should thank Emily for her kindness before he returned to Germany. She'd been one of the few who hadn't judged him because of his accent and had made him feel as though he'd found somewhere he belonged.

Emily looked up in surprise when he entered and gave him a smile. "Your friend isn't with you today?" she asked.

"No.... He...." Jochen pulled himself up sternly. "No, he isn't. Could I have a pot of tea and a scone, please?"

"Of course." Emily glanced at him in some concern, but it was only for a moment. "I'll bring it over in a moment, sir."

Jochen looked around for an empty table and found himself heading for the same one he'd been sitting at when Aiden had come into the tea room. He hesitated but then took a seat there anyway. He was saying goodbye to all of this. This was a part of it.

The tea was placed in front of him. Jochen frowned, noting there were two cups. But before he could comment, Emily walked away to spend a few moments talking to her uncle at the counter. He glanced over at Jochen, eyebrow raised, but nodded in response to whatever Emily said to him.

She brought over the scone he'd ordered, with butter and jam, and then seated herself opposite him. In Aiden's seat.

"You seem to spend more time talking to your customers than working," Jochen said.

"You tend to come in when we're not busy." Emily waited for him to pour his tea, nodding when he offered to pour hers as well. "I assure you I work hard when we are. Oh, and this is my treat. You won't be charged for it."

"There's no need—"

"I disagree." Emily kept her voice light, but he could see her concern. "I've talked to my uncle about it, and he thinks I'm doing the right thing." She stirred her tea, although she hadn't added any sugar. "There's a reason we have an agreement over such things." Something in her tone suggested interrupting would not be a good idea. Besides, Jochen was curious. "After the war, things were... difficult. My cousin had died so wasn't coming home, and my uncle had lost my aunt during the influenza epidemic. Then a lawyer contacted us. An anonymous benefactor had gifted my uncle with enough money to pay all his debts, with quite a bit left over. He and Aunt Mavis had always talked about opening a tea room. It was her dream, and he decided he'd honour it."

"I don't see what this has to do with me," Jochen said. As interesting as her story was, it wasn't exactly relevant.

"It has everything to do with you." Emily smiled. "You asked me when we first met why I listened to you?"

"You did more than that. You were kind." Jochen probably wouldn't have gone back to the theatre that second time if not for her. "You didn't care that I was German, either. I was surprised by that, especially considering you'd lost someone during the war."

"When I came to work for Uncle Vic, we talked about a lot of things. One thing we agreed on was that as someone had been kind to us, for whatever reason, and given our family a second chance, we would pass that kindness on whenever we could." Emily shrugged. "A sympathetic ear to someone who looks as though they need it doesn't cost anything but time, especially when it's quiet here. There are a lot of people who need that now, especially after all the horrible things that have happened over the past few years."

"Isn't that...." Jochen was about to say dangerous, but he wasn't sure that was the right word. "Sometimes men read more into a conversation than is meant."

Emily nodded. "I'm aware of that. I don't talk to everyone, only those I think need some cheering up, and I'm careful and consider myself a good judge of character. As I told you earlier, my uncle is here, and if you tried anything, he'd break your arm as soon as look at you."

"But...."

"Sometimes you have to take chances to do some good." Emily was apparently not to be deterred.

"I'm not so sure about that." Jochen buttered his scone, but found he had no appetite. "Not everything works out so well in practice. I'm starting to wonder if it's better to just not bother in the first place."

"Did something happen?"

"I'm going back to Germany soon." Jochen shrugged. "I'm tired of everyone giving me dirty looks every time I open my mouth. I can take a hint. I know when I'm not wanted."

"What makes you so sure no one wants you here?" Emily seemed surprised. "Mr Foster was very different when he was here with you the other day. I've never seen him that animated before."

"You don't have to lic to make me feel better, although I appreciate you trying."

"It's no lie," Emily said. "He's been coming in here since we opened, and that was the first time anyone has got more than a mumbled couple of words out of him. I had no idea he was the friend you were looking for, as he'd never introduced himself." She frowned. "You said he sang in the theatre? The poor man. I wonder what happened to him."

"The same as to most of us." Despite knowing her words only reflected her concern, Jochen didn't want to discuss Aiden's business with her. "The war."

Was that why Aiden couldn't put any of it behind him? The physical reminders of his voice and limp would bring it back every time he tried to ignore it. Jochen couldn't imagine how difficult that would be. He'd had enough issues working through his own experience without that. What exactly had happened to Aiden during that last battle before he'd been sent home?

Whatever it was, Aiden clearly didn't want any help, or even friendship. He'd made that very clear by his reaction.

Then why had he told Jochen he wanted to be friends when they'd first met in the tea room?

"I don't suppose he's been in here since last Wednesday?" Jochen asked her. He tried to remember whether he'd mentioned the name of his hotel to Aiden. The tea room might be somewhere he'd come to find Jochen if he changed his mind.

"I'm sorry, no." Emily sipped her tea, and they sat in silence for a few minutes. "I should get back to work. Will you be in here again before you return home?"

"Probably not, no." Jochen pondered aloud. "I need to pack up my great-aunt's cottage, so I'll probably leave from there." There was no point in continuing to pay for a hotel when he could stay at the cottage. He inclined his head towards her. "Thank you for your kindness, Emily. I wish you well." A thought occurred to him. "I never introduced myself properly, did I? I'm Jochen Weber."

"Emily Riley." Emily smiled. "I'll leave you to finish your tea in peace. It's been a pleasure talking with you, Mr Weber. I hope you have a good trip home to Germany and that you find whatever it is you're looking for."

"You're not sleeping well, lad?"

Aiden looked up in surprise.

"Less than usual that is?" Jack added before Aiden had the chance to answer the first question.

"Maybe." Although Aiden had never been able to fool Jack about anything, he wasn't sure he wanted to admit the truth this time.

"That's what I thought." Jack stopped sweeping and took a seat on the chest Aiden used as a toolbox. He patted the spot next to him, but Aiden stayed where he was. "Sometimes all of us need to get whatever's troubling us off our chest. Even you."

"I don't—"

"Talk? That you do, lad. More than you realise." Jack fixed his gaze on Aiden, who stared back, determined not to flinch. "Just because you don't say the words out loud doesn't mean they're not there and being spoken in some other way. I've worked in this theatre a long time, long enough to know that not all the dramas are played out on stage. Usually the really important ones aren't." His eyes narrowed. "That German bloke didn't upset you, did he?"

"No," Aiden said quickly. "Jochen... Mr Weber was very kind to me." That was the problem. Jochen had been very kind. But more than that, he'd seemed to understand Aiden better than anyone else ever had.

"Good." Jack relaxed a bit. "Something's upset you, though. You've got dark circles around your eyes, and you're jumping at every little noise, worse than you were when you first got back."

"I'm not sleeping," Aiden confirmed. If he went along with the conversation, Jack might back off and leave him alone. "Sometimes... sometimes the nightmares are worse."

"I remember when you first came here," Jack said. "After the war, I mean. I remember what you were like before that too." He smiled as though visualising a memory.

"That stage was everything to you. You used to lose yourself in it, and sometimes I wondered if that was really a good thing. A man's got to find himself before he can lose himself in a role."

Jack had a tendency towards insightfulness. There were rumours he'd been an educated man, but something had happened to him to make him turn his back on all of it.

"You don't think I ever found myself, is that it?" Aiden spoke his thoughts aloud before he realised what he'd done.

"You're a bright lad, Aiden, but you've been through far more than a man should." Jack removed his hat and studied it, running his fingers over the brim. "War's a terrible thing, that it is. It leaves its mark on a man, and no amount of scrubbing gets rid of it. Some men learn to live with it. Others don't. The secret is to find something or someone who makes you forget. Even for a short time. You don't want to forget it forever, that's just as bad."

"That sounds like the voice of experience." Aiden had used music to forget. It had worked for a while, but now that Jochen had returned, it no longer did. "You didn't fight in the war, did you?"

Surely he would have been too old to enlist?

"Maybe not in your war, but there's always been one somewhere or another. They're all as bad as each other, although with each new one, people often forget what came before. They're fools."

"You're more than you appear to be, Jack."

"And you're more than you let yourself be." Jack stood and shoved his hat back onto his head. "This theatre isn't going to sweep itself." He picked up his broom and studied Aiden for a moment. "I had a son once, you know. You remind me of him. He was a stubborn one, too, just like you. I didn't get the chance to say a lot of what I should have to him. We think we have all the time in the world to say what needs to be said, but we don't. Remember that."

"I'm sorry," Aiden started to say, but Jack had already turned his back and walked away. He had a tendency to dish out words of wisdom and then disappear before he could be asked any questions.

Despite what he'd told Jack, Aiden knew full well why he wasn't sleeping. He missed Jochen, his easy companionship, and their conversation. Their last goodbye replayed through his mind. Although he'd turned his back quickly and walked away, Aiden had still seen the hurt in Jochen's eyes. Jochen had been kind to him, and Aiden had repaid him by being a cad.

He'd behaved that way because of his own fears, because of the more than friendship he suspected he felt for Jochen. Jochen had done nothing untoward. All he'd done was offer the friendship Aiden had later thrown back at him, and that was after telling Jochen that yes, he did want to be friends. He'd talked to Jochen more than he had to anyone in years. For those hours they'd spent together, Aiden had almost forgotten the hoarseness of his voice and his limp. For the first time since the war, he'd wanted to talk instead of keeping to himself and hoping no one noticed. His desire for conversation had overcome his fear.

Jochen was only in the country a short time. What would it matter if Aiden accepted his friendship while he was here? Surely Aiden owed him that much for the kindness he'd shown? If Jochen wanted to stay in contact afterward, they could correspond through letters. Aiden wouldn't have to see him again, feel his touch, and wonder what it would be like to have more.

Words on a page were safe. They'd be miles away, on different continents.

I miss you.

Had Jochen mentioned a date by which he had to return to Germany? Bloody hell. Why couldn't Aiden remember? He couldn't even remember the hotel Jochen was staying at.

He grabbed his coat. Now the decision was made, he didn't want to waste time in pursuing it. The girl at the tea room might know where to find Jochen. They'd seemed friendly, and Jochen had referred to her by her first name.

Aiden slapped his hand to his forehead. God, he was so stupid. That was why Jochen had picked the tea room to meet. He and Emily were probably courting, or at least spending time together. It made so much sense. Much more than the foolish musing of a man thinking another man might be interested in him.

His old walking stick caught his attention. It stood in the corner, discarded but not completely. Aiden picked it up. If he had to walk to Jochen's hotel, he had no clue how far it was. He wasn't going to let his stupid leg slow him down and prevent him from doing what needed to be done.

It didn't take as long as he thought it would to reach his destination, but even so Aiden was glad when the journey was over. He took a few deep breaths, hoped he didn't look as nervous as he felt, and pushed open the tea room door.

Emily looked up at the sound of the bell. She smiled at him, although Aiden had no idea why. If Jochen had talked to her about him, surely her response would have been somewhat chilly? He doubted she'd help him, but he was determined to ask her about Jochen anyway.

"Good afternoon, Emily," he said, trying his best to be polite and make conversation. He ignored the urge to turn around and stride out the way he'd come. "Have you seen Jochen... Mr Weber today?"

"Good afternoon, Mr Foster." Emily looked at him for a moment as though he'd suddenly sprouted another head, but she quickly regained her composure. "Not today, but he was in here yesterday." Her smile grew wider. "He was asking after you, actually."

"After me?" Aiden spluttered. He swallowed and forced himself to continue. "I don't suppose you know where he is?"

"You're very polite today, Mr Foster."

Damn it. She was going to make him work for it. He had been rather rude to her in the past, so he deserved it, he supposed.

"Thank you for noticing, Miss...." Aiden realised he didn't know her surname, hadn't even known her first name until Jochen had told him.

"Miss Riley." Emily kept her tone light, but it was impossible to miss the amusement in it. "I thought you didn't believe in miracles, and yet here you are performing a minor one."

"It's still about four weeks until Christmas," Aiden countered. "Are you going to tell me where Jochen is or not?"

"He mentioned something about packing up his great aunt's cottage," Emily said after a few moments. "I'm not sure whether he'd still be there, though. He also said he was returning home to Germany soon."

"Oh." Aiden hoped he hadn't already left it too late. He glanced at the grandfather clock in the corner of the room. If he left now, he might make the next train to Crayford and be at the cottage before dark. The hotel had rooms where he could stay if he missed the last train back to London. "Thank you."

"You're welcome."

He tipped his hat to her and headed out the door.

Jochen jumped at the knock at the door, although it wasn't very loud. For a moment he thought he'd imagined it, but then whoever it was knocked again.

Had Mrs Grant forgotten something? She'd only left ten minutes before, having called in to share some anecdotes about Great-aunt Wilhelmina as she'd promised. It was an interesting hour or so, and she was happy to chat for as long as he continued to supply decent cups of tea. He'd come to the cottage with enough supplies for several days, so doing so wasn't a problem. His great-aunt had had a good sense of humour and was what Mrs Grant referred to as rather a free spirit. She'd also had a decent amount of common sense and a willingness to put aside convention in favour of making sure people had what they needed to be happy. Apparently she'd not been above the odd bit of matchmaking either, although that particular attribute had made Great-uncle Jeremy roll his eyes affectionately on more than one occasion. Mrs Grant had spoken of her fondly. She'd been well liked and would be missed.

Jochen still wasn't sure why he'd decided to stay awhile longer in Crayford. It wasn't just to sort through his great-aunt's possessions. Although he'd never known her, being here gave him a sense of belonging, of being home, that he no longer felt in Germany since his father had died. He wasn't sure what that said about him, clinging to the stories of what was left of family, of a woman who probably hadn't known he existed. After all, her will had named Jochen's father as her heir. Not him.

He'd lost so many people. Sometimes he wondered if

the hole they'd left would ever be filled. At least Great-aunt Wilhelmina had had her Jeremy. But at what cost? She'd lost her family. Perhaps by being here, he could make that right and fool himself that it wasn't already too late.

He put down the book he was leafing through and called out, "I'm coming." He'd left the door unlocked, but either the person on the other side hadn't realised or was too polite to push it open and come in.

The last person he expected to see stood outside. "Can I come in?" Aiden asked. His shoulders were hunched, and he was leaning on a cane. "I'll understand if you'd prefer I didn't."

"Nonsense," Jochen said, quick to reassure him. He stood aside to let Aiden enter. "It's good to see you. Please, come in."

Aiden limped inside. "Do you mind if I sit?" he asked. "I had to run for the train in London, and my blasted leg is still protesting." He lowered himself onto the sofa.

"You ran?" Jochen couldn't help but sound incredulous.

"Limped very quickly, then," Aiden amended, a rueful look on his face. "It's not something I tend to do often, but...." He shrugged.

"I was about to make more tea. Would you like some?" The last thing on Jochen's mind was tea, but it would give him some time to recover his composure. Aiden was breathing heavily, and he was flushed. It was very endearing. "Can I take your hat and coat? You are staying, aren't you?"

"You're babbling, Jochen." Aiden smiled. There was amusement in his voice. That and nervousness. "I'd like some tea. I can stay awhile." He hesitated. "If you'd like me to."

"I'd like you to." Jochen took Aiden's coat and hat and

hung them on the stand by the door. "I'll make some tea, and then we can talk."

Whatever had brought Aiden here, Jochen was determined to make sure he left on better terms than their last meeting. Or at the very least, come to a mutual agreement as to whether to continue their friendship or not. If Aiden had come to say goodbye properly, then Jochen would adhere to it, but he wanted their last time together to be a good memory.

He glanced into the living room. Aiden was holding something around his neck, his fingers caressing it absently. He still wore his button. That had to be a good thing. Right?

"Here you are." Jochen put the tea tray down on the occasional table and took a seat on the sofa opposite. He didn't trust himself to sit too close. Keeping his distance would help him stay composed. The last thing he wanted was to scare Aiden off.

Was that what had happened last time?

"Look, there's no need to be embarrassed over what happened last time," Jochen blurted out. "I'm the last person who is going to hold that kind of thing against you. I understand. Really. I went through horrible things during the war too." He added hurriedly, "I'm not saying they were worse, but...."

"Slow down." Aiden held up one hand. "I'm not going anywhere. You don't have to get an hour's conversation into ten minutes." He poured himself some tea. His hand shook as he added milk and then placed the cup and saucer back on the tray. "I owe you an apology. I've been an absolute cad. You were being kind, and I was rude." He sighed. "You don't know me that well. I'm not always that easy to get along with. It's been so long since I've bothered to make the effort with anyone that I suspect I've forgotten how."

"You don't owe me anything." Jochen noticed Aiden's voice was stronger than he'd heard it since they'd found each other again. The hoarseness was still there, but not so obvious. For a moment he'd almost sounded like his old self again.

"I'm trying to apologise. Humour me."

"All right." Jochen held out his hand. "Apology accepted."

"Thank you." Aiden gripped Jochen's hand firmly and shook it. "I missed you. And not just because you were kind."

"I missed you too." Jochen noticed Aiden was still holding his hand. His skin was warm against Jochen's. More than that, it felt good.

Aiden suddenly blushed and pulled away. "I suppose you're going back to Germany in a few days." He cleared his throat. "If you'd still like to be friends, I'd like that too. I thought... perhaps we could spend some time together, and then... I could write to you."

"I'd still like to." Jochen found Aiden's flushed skin rather arousing. This wouldn't do at all. The last thing he needed was to ruin what he'd almost lost. "I must warn you, though, that my handwriting is appalling. But if you're prepared to decipher it, I'll definitely write to you."

"I'm prepared to." Aiden picked up his cup and sipped his tea.

"Good. It's settled, then." Jochen poured his own tea and added a couple of spoonfuls of sugar. He could do this. He could focus on the friendship Aiden seemed to want and ignore any inappropriate thoughts and feelings. A thought occurred to him. "How did you find me?"

"Emily... Miss Riley... told me you'd be here." Aiden looked up at Jochen, a horrified look on his face. "Oh, Lord.

No, I didn't go to the tea room just to see her. I went looking for you. I don't have any intentions towards your sweetheart."

Jochen spluttered tea and nearly dropped his cup. "Huh?" He gazed at Aiden in total disbelief.

What on earth had given him the idea that Emily was Jochen's sweetheart?

CHAPTER EIGHT

"Aiden won't be long." Old Jack eyed Jochen with some degree of suspicion. "I thought you would have gone back to Germany by now."

"I haven't quite finished my business in London," Jochen said. "I haven't decided yet whether or not I'm going to return home."

He and Aiden had been meeting regularly for several weeks now, and Jochen was no longer sure he wanted to return to Germany. The longer he stayed here and spent time with Aiden, the more it felt like he was where he was supposed to be. He'd moved into Lavender Cottage and was beginning to get to know the villagers. Despite some of them being unsure of what to make of a stranger in their midst, and a German at that, most of them were beginning to thaw somewhat. Jochen was sure the Grants had put in a good word for him, and Great-aunt Wilhelmina's reputation hadn't done any harm either.

Jack's expression softened a little. "Young Aiden looks more like his old self this past month than he has since he got back from the front. Having a friend is good for him."

He cocked his head to the side. "Does he know you're thinking about staying?"

"Not yet," Jochen admitted. "I'm looking into some courses at the university. I should find out soon. I didn't want to say anything until I knew for certain." Thanks to his inheritance, there was no longer the same urgency to get home and find work. He'd always wanted to study English literature seriously, and the opportunity to do so was very tempting. The added incentive of spending more time with Aiden didn't hurt either.

"Good idea." Jack sounded as though he approved, and his tone was almost friendly.

"You've known Aiden a long time," Jochen began cautiously.

"That I have." Jack apparently was not about to volunteer information that readily.

"I met him briefly early on in the war." Jochen wasn't sure there was another way to ask what he needed to know. "I'm concerned about him, and I'd like to help if I can."

Jack's eyes narrowed. "Poking around isn't going to."

"You said having a friend is good for him." Jochen tried again. "I don't mean him any harm. I... do you know what happened to him over there? He won't talk about it."

"If he won't talk about it, it might mean he doesn't want to." Jack looked thoughtful. "Or maybe he feels he can't."

"That's my thought too." This was the first decent conversation Jochen had had with Jack. Aiden had told him there was more to the old man than met the eye. It appeared he was right. "If he feels I'm pushing him, he'll run. I don't want that, although I can understand why. I have memories I don't want to think about too."

"Everyone who fights in a war has, lad," Jack said. "So do people who haven't. It's part of life."

"I just want to know how to help him."

"I can see that." Jack actually smiled. "Are you asking me for advice?"

"Yes." Jochen didn't see the point in denying it. "You know him better than I do, and he speaks highly of you."

"You don't need to resort to flattery, lad." Jack took off his cap and studied it for a moment before putting it back on. "I owe you an apology. I was rude to you when we first met."

"Yes, you were." Jochen wasn't about to deny it. "And I'm not trying to flatter you. I'm merely speaking the truth."

Jack's eyes twinkled. "I'm thinking I might have misjudged you, but then you probably thought I was a cantankerous old man." He grinned. "You'd be right about that."

"You were going to give me some advice?"

"Was I?" Jack began sweeping again. "Goodness, will you look at the time. I'll be in trouble for not doing my job at this rate." He turned to leave.

Jochen caught him by the shoulder. "Please, Jack. I don't know what to do, and I'm worried about him."

"Don't be, lad. Keep being his friend, and he'll find the right path eventually. Be there when he needs you, and be patient." Jack tapped the side of his nose. "Good things take time, as the saying goes. You're young, and so is he. You've still got time on your side, but don't leave it too late, mind. Sometimes things need to be said, and it's the only way."

Jochen frowned. "What do you mean by...?" But Jack was already gone. Surely he couldn't be referring to...?

The one thing Jochen wanted to tell Aiden, needed to tell him, was the one thing he couldn't. The longer he spent with Aiden, the more Jochen realised that what he felt for his friend was much more than that.

He was falling in love with Aiden. And it was getting harder not to say anything. But he couldn't ruin their friendship by telling him. Especially as Aiden had shown no sign he felt the same way.

~

"You don't need to walk me home, Jochen." Aiden voiced his protest because he thought he should, but secretly he was pleased Jochen was doing so.

"And miss out on a decent cup of tea and a slice of Mrs Hamilton's fruitcake?" Jochen chuckled. "I think not, and besides I want to meet her."

"She wants to meet you too," Aiden said. Maybe she wouldn't interrogate Jochen *too* much. She'd been curious about Jochen for a while, but Aiden had put off introducing the two of them. He still wasn't sure where he stood with Jochen, especially as it wouldn't be much longer before Jochen had to return to Germany, as he'd already put it off longer than Aiden expected. He hoped they'd at least get to spend Christmas together, especially as they'd originally met at that time six years ago.

"I enjoyed the film." Jochen had his hands stuffed in his pockets, although it wasn't that cold and he was wearing gloves. "Unfortunately, though, I haven't read *Bleak House*, and now I know what happens."

"Oh." Aiden hoped he didn't sound as mortified as he felt. "Jochen, you should have said something! There were other films playing we could have seen. I chose this one because I know how much you love Dickens."

"I'm only teasing, Aiden." Jochen grinned. "Besides, now I have all that wonderful dialogue to look forward to. They can only fit so much on the placards, and now I know what the characters look like." His voice grew wistful. "I wish I could have heard what they sounded like."

"Perhaps one day they'll show films with sound." Aiden had read there had been some success with very short segments, but so far nothing longer. Hopefully there had been further advancement he hadn't heard of yet, so it was closer to becoming reality than he thought. "But in the meantime you can always imagine that part of it when you read the book. It's one you don't have yet, isn't it?"

"I don't have it," Jochen confirmed. "I'm slowly building a collection of books in English, and Great-aunt Wilhelmina had a decent-sized library. It is very difficult to find English language books in Germany, so this is a real treat."

"From what you've told me of her, she reminds me of you." Aiden made a mental note to find a copy of *Bleak House* for Jochen's collection.

"Really?" Jochen sounded pleased at the comparison. "Mrs Grant said the same thing the other day, but you know me better than she does."

Aiden flushed at the comment but hoped Jochen hadn't noticed. "She was fond of her literature too."

"That's all?" Jochen looked disappointed. "I thought you were going to talk about my wit and charm." He put on an expression that reminded Aiden of a puppy. "Don't tell me I have none!"

"You have a strange sense of humour at times, Jochen." Aiden enjoyed the light banter between them. It tended to enter into most conversations they had. "Of course you're charming, although some might say extremely charming would be considered a hyperbole."

"A hyperbole? Really?" Jochen laughed. "I obviously need to work on my charm, then, don't I?" He nearly lost his footing on a rough section of the road. "Some? Only some?"

"Only some." Aiden steadied Jochen, catching him before he fell. They stood looking at each other, Aiden's hands on Jochen's shoulders. Time seemed to slow. Aiden could feel Jochen's breath on his skin. He loosened his grip on Jochen and moved back quickly, sliding his cane off his arm into his hand. "Perhaps if you took your hands out of your pockets, you'd be steadier on your feet."

Jochen seemed a little dazed. He licked his lips. "Perhaps," he said slowly. "Wait a minute. That makes no sense at all. Does it?"

"It's all about balance." Aiden thought Jochen came out with the strangest things at times, but it was part of what Aiden liked about him. Sometimes he caught Jochen daydreaming, the sweetest smile on his lips. But when Jochen noticed Aiden looking at him, he returned to reality very quickly and refused to say what he'd been thinking about. There was a bit of that about him now.

"I'm sorry, I was thinking about something else entirely."

"I guessed as much." Aiden shook his head. "It's good for a man to dream, Jochen, but not when you're crossing a road." He waited for Jochen to catch up. "We're almost there."

"You move quite quickly with that cane of yours."

"Practice." Aiden had started using it again since that day at the cottage. He didn't need it at the theatre, but Jochen liked to walk, and Aiden didn't want to slow him down.

"It gives you something of a distinguished air."

"You mean it makes it easier for you to pretend I'm a gentleman?"

"You are a gentleman, Aiden." Jochen sounded so serious that Aiden turned to look at him, but his expression seemed sincere. "Any... any woman would be privileged to be on your arm."

I'm not interested in any woman.

Aiden felt a pang of disappointment at Jochen's words. Despite his intentions to keep their relationship as one of close friendship, and disregard his fantasies for the foolish things they were, he still wondered what it would be like to have Jochen on his arm. Or better yet, in his arms, holding him close and kissing him.

But even *if* Jochen did return Aiden's feelings, it would never be something they could do. At least in public.

"If you say so," Aiden mumbled, relieved that his lodgings were around the next corner. As they turned it, he saw the curtain fall back quickly from the front window. Mrs Hamilton was apparently looking out for them.

He reached inside his pocket for his key but didn't need it, as the door wasn't locked. "After you," he told Jochen after opening the door. "Can I take your coat and hat?"

"Thank you." Jochen looked around with interest while Aiden hung up their coats and hats.

It was a modest house, a bit on the small side but a little bigger than Lavender Cottage. Photographs of the late Mr Hamilton adorned the walls of the hallway, some of him alone, others with his wife, taken at various stages of their life together. There also photographs of Aiden's parents, and one of Aiden with them as a small child.

Aiden noticed Jochen peering at that particular photograph, his brow creased in concentration. "Yes, that is me. Mrs Hamilton has been a family friend for as long as I can remember. She and my mother were more like sisters than close friends."

"I thought it was you. I recognized that intense expression you get sometimes." Jochen glanced at Aiden and then back at the photograph. "And these are your parents?"

"Yes."

"Aiden, aren't you going to introduce me to your friend?" Mrs Hamilton's question took Aiden by surprise. He hadn't seen her standing in the doorway. How long had she been there watching them? When she hadn't appeared immediately as he'd entered the house, he'd presumed she was busy in the kitchen.

"Mrs Hamilton, this is my good friend Jochen Weber." Aiden nodded to Jochen. "Jochen, this is Mrs Hamilton."

"It's a pleasure to meet you, Mrs Hamilton." Jochen gave her a slight bow. "Aiden has spoken highly of you."

Mrs Hamilton flushed slightly, but rapidly regained her composure. "It's nice to finally meet you too, Mr Weber. I'm so glad Aiden has made a friend. He's needed that for a while."

Aiden cleared his throat, reminding them both he was there and listening to the conversation. "I've told Jochen about your fruitcake, Mrs Hamilton."

"I'm looking forward to having some," Jochen added quickly.

"I've made some tea. Please come and sit down." Mrs Hamilton gestured them to come into the sitting room. She took a seat on the chair by the fire, which left the sofa free for Jochen and Aiden.

Aiden swallowed. The sofa wasn't that big, but there wasn't the option of another chair. There was no way they'd be able to share it without sitting very close. He still felt off-kilter from having stopped Jochen from losing his footing. He wanted to touch him again, although he knew he shouldn't. The last thing he needed was a dose of reality to help his imagination where his dreams were concerned.

They were very nice dreams, but ones he knew he shouldn't be having.

Jochen sat first and took the cup of tea Mrs Hamilton offered him. "This is very kind of you, Mrs Hamilton, thank you."

"How much longer will you be staying in London, Mr Weber? I've asked Aiden, but he doesn't seem to know." She frowned in Aiden's direction. "Sit down, Aiden. You're hovering, and your tea will be getting cold. You know you don't like cold tea."

"He's already stayed much longer than he intended," Aiden said. He sat down carefully, squeezing himself into the corner of the sofa. His knee brushed against Jochen's, despite Aiden's best intentions to avoid touching him.

"I'm not sure." Jochen helped himself to a slice of fruit-cake when Mrs Hamilton offered him one. He seemed oblivious as to how close he and Aiden were sitting. "My great-aunt's affairs have taken longer to sort out than I anticipated. I should know before Christmas."

"You'll be here for Christmas, then?" Mrs Hamilton asked before Aiden could. "You must come here for Christmas dinner, Mr Weber. Unless you have other plans?"

"That sounds wonderful, Mrs Hamilton, thank you." Jochen smiled and took a bite of fruitcake. "This cake is delicious, and if I'm to come for Christmas please call me Jochen."

"It's settled, then." Mrs Hamilton looked pleased. "Won't that be nice, Aiden?"

"Oh, yes. Very nice." Aiden plastered on a smile. A

flutter of excitement warmed the pit of his stomach, but it was quickly followed by a sinking feeling.

As much as he wanted Jochen to stay for as long as he could, the more time they spent together, the harder it became for Aiden to hide his feelings towards him.

Jochen knocked firmly on Mrs Hamilton's front door. He'd spent most of the walk there trying to come up with an excuse as to why he was visiting on his own. Pretending he'd lost his hat was an option he'd quickly dismissed. He wanted to talk to her, and for her to trust him, so she felt comfortable telling him what he needed to know. Starting the conversation with a lie seemed wrong in that context. In any context really.

It had been a couple of days since he'd met her, but that afternoon tea was still clear in his mind. Not so much for the conversation, but the fact that he'd had to sit so close to Aiden while trying to avoid touching him. It had been torture, to say the least, especially when Aiden had brushed his leg against Jochen's.

Jochen's heart had sped up. He'd resisted the urge to wipe his damp palms on his trousers. Aiden, however, hadn't seemed to notice, which was one small mercy. Jochen hoped he hadn't sounded too inane in his conversation, but he'd needed to focus on small talk in order to keep his composure. He'd been torn when Mrs Hamilton had invited him for Christmas dinner, but his acceptance was out of his mouth before he could stop it.

Aiden's response had sounded forced. Jochen hoped he wasn't intruding, despite the invitation. He'd debated talking to Aiden about it, but the right moment to do so hadn't presented itself as yet. From what he could see, Mrs Hamilton was the closest thing Aiden had left of family, and Jochen didn't want to be there if he wasn't wanted.

"Hello, Mr Weber." Mrs Hamilton smiled when she opened the door and saw him, but there was also a mix of concern and surprise in her expression. "Can I help you, dear? Aiden's not here. He's at work."

"Jochen," Jochen corrected gently. "Actually it was you I came to see. Can I come in?"

Mrs Hamilton stood to one side to let him in. "Is everything all right? You seem a little flushed. You're not feeling poorly, are you?"

"No, I'm fine. Thank you for asking." Jochen handed her his coat and hat when she offered to hang them up for him and then followed her into the sitting room.

"Would you like some tea?"

"That sounds wonderful. Thank you." Jochen sat down on the sofa, the same one he'd shared with Aiden the other day. He'd have to be careful as to what he said. Despite her kindness towards him, he doubted Mrs Hamilton would be very sympathetic if she discovered his true feelings for Aiden.

There was a book lying on the occasional table at the side of the sofa. He picked it up and opened it, smiling when he recognized the words within. "I didn't know you liked to read Dickens, Mrs Hamilton," he said when she returned with a tea tray.

"Oh, that's Aiden's," she said, after he took the tray from her and laid it down on the table. "He loves to read, and for some reason has a fondness for that particular book. It's one he rereads frequently."

"*David Copperfield*," Jochen said softly. It was the only Dickens book Aiden had told him he'd read when they'd first met. Jochen had his own copy. It was worn and well-read, even more so since that day as it now had the added appeal of reminding him of his first conversation with Aiden.

Mrs Hamilton had provided more of the delicious fruit-cake with the tea. Jochen took a slice when it was offered and munched slowly, trying to get his thoughts together. There was only one thing for it. He'd have to get straight to the point.

"I'm here because I'm worried about Aiden," he said once he'd finished eating.

"I wondered if that were the case." Mrs Hamilton sipped her tea. "You've come to ask me about him, haven't you?"

"So my misguided attempt to be subtle about leading the conversation in that direction was doomed to fail before it began?"

"Yes." She chuckled. "You've been good for Aiden. He was always such a quiet boy, despite his gift. He gets that from Molly, you know. His mother. She had a beautiful singing voice and loved her music too. His personality, though, that's more Harold. He was a quiet man, very intense. They were very much in love. I remember her telling him she'd found the right man after their first meeting."

Jochen could understand that. While he hadn't known Aiden was the man he wanted when they'd first met, he certainly knew it now. If only things were as simple for them as they'd been for Aiden's parents.

"Aiden has a beautiful voice." Jochen didn't want to refer to it in past tense as that would be admitting it was lost forever. "I heard him sing when we first met. The memory has stayed with me ever since."

"It's a shame what happened to him." Mrs Hamilton shook her head and put her cup and saucer back on the tray. "He hasn't told you?"

"He won't talk about it," Jochen said. "He gets agitated every time I try, and I don't want to upset him." He took a deep breath, the words falling from him in a rush. "I want to help him, to give him back what he's lost. I'm not sure his voice is completely gone. I notice when he gets passionate about something there's an echo there of what it used to be like. He forgets where and when he is, and everything he's gone through, and his voice grows stronger."

"That's interesting." Mrs Hamilton seemed thoughtful. It was a few minutes before she spoke again. Jochen didn't interrupt, figuring she'd continue when she was ready. "I pride myself in being a decent judge of character, Mr Weber... Jochen, and I believe you truly care for Aiden and want what is best for him."

Jochen nodded. His mouth was dry. He wanted to tell her that yes, he did, but he couldn't find the sound to make the words.

"I'm also not entirely sure that he won't break through whatever is holding him back without some effort," she said. "Sometimes we have to be cruel to be kind, you know?"

"I couldn't be cruel to Aiden." Jochen protested the thought, although a little voice in the back of his mind reminded him that he probably already had, because he'd offered friendship and secretly wanted more. So much more that he'd got into the habit of walking with his hands in his pockets whenever they were out together. He'd found himself close to slipping his hand into Aiden's, and that wouldn't do at all, however much he wanted it. Not only would it horrify Aiden, but it would also get both of them into a great deal of trouble.

"He's going to miss you when you return to Germany." Mrs Hamilton focused her gaze on him. He struggled not to flinch. She would be a difficult person to hide something from.

"I know. I'm going to miss him too. He's a good friend."

Mrs Hamilton seemed to relax. She leaned back in her chair and redirected her gaze to the fire. "Molly told me what the doctors said about Aiden. He doesn't know I know, and I don't want him to. If I repeat it, and I'm only doing so because if anyone can get through to the boy, I think it might be you. Promise me this stays between us?"

"You have my word."

"You know he was wounded?" Mrs Hamilton continued after Jochen nodded. "Two bullets in the leg, which is why he limps now. The doctors say he was lucky not to lose it. He was found lying in the mud on the edge of a shell hole, dead bodies on either side of him. He was soaking wet and running a fever."

"I knew he'd been shot," Jochen said softly, "but not the rest."

"It took months before he spoke again, and then when he did, it was with that horrible hoarse whisper he uses now." Mrs Hamilton sighed. "I try not to notice it, but some days I just want to cry. He's lost so much. Firstly, to go through all that, and then both his parents dying of the influenza. I took him in afterwards. It was the least I could do. Not just for him, but for them."

"Do the doctors know why he lost his voice?" Jochen asked.

"No. They say there is no reason he shouldn't speak normally. They can't find a reason for it. One of them called it hysteria."

"Does he know that?"

"Oh, yes, but knowing it and fixing it are two different things. The doctors said it should come back in time, but it hasn't. Four years later and it hasn't. He still has nightmares. I've heard him scream in his sleep, and he wouldn't be able to do that if his voice was damaged, would he?"

"I'm sorry," Jochen said softly. "This must be very difficult for you, telling me this."

She wiped at her eyes. "Remember your promise. He's not to know we've spoken about this."

"I'll remember." Jochen averted his gaze. He'd intruded into something private with someone he barely knew. Despite the fact it had been her decision to tell him, he wondered whether he had the right to bring up what were so obviously painful memories.

This war, and everything that had come with it, had taken so much from so many.

"Would you like me to go?" Jochen asked. "I can make you a fresh pot of tea before I do if you'd like me to."

"You're a kind man, Jochen." Mrs Hamilton managed a shaky smile. "A fresh pot of tea is a wonderful idea, but please stay awhile. I'd like to talk about happier times. There are stories about Molly and her boys that shouldn't be lost. I'd like them to be remembered the way they were, and I'm not sure Aiden will ever speak of them."

"I hope he will one day." Jochen picked up the tray. "You sit there, and I'll make us some more tea. I can stay awhile, but I'd like to be gone before Aiden gets home."

"Yes, yes, of course. It would be awkward if he found us talking, especially as you were never here."

"Of course, that's right." Jochen remembered where the kitchen was from his last visit. "I was never here."

CHAPTER NINE

Aiden drummed his fingers on the neatly wrapped package on the table in front of him, the rhythm a mixture of different lines from various songs. Songs he'd once sung as part of the theatre, but of late had begun replaying in his mind. Occasionally he'd even find himself humming them under his breath, surprised when he caught himself doing so.

He glanced out the window of the tea house for the fifth time in as many minutes. Where was Jochen? He was late, and Jochen was never late. Had something happened to him? Oh Lord, no. Aiden suddenly had a vision of Jochen crumpled in the middle of the road, bleeding, after stepping out without watching where he was going.

Or in bed with a fever, his brow damp with perspiration, his nightclothes clinging to him....

Stop it. That last one, in particular, was not somewhere he needed to go at the moment. At any moment.

The bell rang over the door. Jochen strode in, looking around the room. He smiled when he saw Aiden and sat down in the seat opposite. It was their usual table, the one that was always free when they needed it.

Emily barely hid a grin from behind the counter. She'd commented on Aiden's nervousness, teasing him about it. Aiden suspected she'd reserved that table for them on the days they frequented the tea room. He and Jochen were creatures of habit, meeting there regularly for lunch on Wednesdays and Fridays.

"I'm sorry I'm late, but I have news!" Jochen sounded excited. He placed his hat on the table and ran his hand through his hair.

"You're not that late," Aiden said. "I haven't been here long. What's happened? You're all right, aren't you?"

He heard Emily giggle and scowled at her, but Jochen seemed unaware of the interruption or Aiden's response to it.

"I'm fine," Jochen said. "More than fine. As I said, I have news." He leaned in closer. "I've been accepted for an English literature course at the university. It starts in the new year, so...."

"You don't need to go back to Germany," Aiden finished slowly. "Jochen, that's great news." It was, wasn't it? He was in no hurry to lose Jochen's company, although as their friendship grew Aiden knew he couldn't continue to hide his feelings for him much longer.

"You don't mind, do you?" Jochen suddenly seemed anxious, subdued, as though the thought had only just occurred to him. "I mean, this was supposed to just be temporary. We were going to correspond once I got hom—back to Germany."

"Of course I don't mind, silly." Aiden reached across the table and grabbed Jochen's hand in his own without thinking. "We're friends, aren't we? I like spending time with you. Besides, who else would you talk to about everything you're going to study?"

Even as he said the words, his heart sank. If Jochen was taking classes at the university, he'd have others to talk to about his love of literature. Others who were more learned than Aiden. How long would it be before Jochen found new friends and didn't need their regular meetings anymore?

Jochen stared at his hand in Aiden's. He swallowed. "Yes, we're friends. Of course we are."

"Oh, sorry." Aiden snatched his hand away quickly and shoved it in his lap. "Sorry," he repeated. "I wasn't thinking." He blushed, a slow warmth disappearing underneath his shirt collar. "Actually, I have something for you. I was going to wait until a bit later to give it to you, but considering your news, this is the right time."

He handed Jochen the package. Jochen gave him a questioning look. "What is this?"

"Open it and find out," Aiden suggested. "Consider it an early Christmas present." He hadn't wanted to wait until Saturday to give it to Jochen, particularly because of what it was. This was something personal between himself and Jochen, and selfishly, he didn't want to share Jochen's reaction with Mrs Hamilton.

"I...." Jochen seemed rather taken aback. "Thank you, Aiden. You didn't need to get me anything."

"I wanted to," Aiden said. Seeing Jochen flustered like this was very endearing. Rather too much so. Aiden busied himself pouring them both some tea. "Open it first before you thank me."

What if Jochen had already purchased a copy? Had Aiden left it too late? His mouth went dry. His hand shook.

"Oh, goodness." Jochen ripped off the paper and ran his fingers over the front of the book. "It's *Bleak House*. My very own copy of *Bleak House*." He opened it and read the inscription to himself, his lips moving with the words.

"You don't already have it?" Aiden asked. It had taken him a long time to work out how to inscribe it. There was so much he wanted to say to Jochen and couldn't.

"No." Jochen grinned from ear to ear. "Oh, Aiden, this is the best Christmas present I've ever been given. I shall treasure it always." He reread the inscription again, this time aloud. "To my dear friend, Jochen. Warm regards, Aiden."

"Just make sure you read it," Aiden said, knowing full well Jochen would and more than once. "Books are meant to be read as well as treasured."

"Of course. That goes without saying," Jochen said. He placed the book reverently on the table; his gaze kept going back to it. He wet his lips with his tongue. "I have a surprise for you too."

"A surprise? What kind of surprise?" Aiden put down his tea. "Your news is wonderful." He sighed and stared into his cup. "It's wonderful."

Why on earth did Jochen want to stay? Surely there were similar courses available in Germany? Jochen already had a degree. He'd been offered a teaching position in Berlin.

"I'm not staying just because I want to study English literature," Jochen said softly. "Your friendship means a great deal to me, Aiden. I'm not ready to give it up yet and go back to Germany."

"You wouldn't have to give it up," Aiden said. Not ready yet? How long would it be before he was? "We could correspond. We already said that."

"Yes, but I'd miss our conversations." Jochen lightened his tone, but his voice sounded strained. "It's not the same as having one like we are now. I'd have to wait forever for your replies, and you'd have to decipher my handwriting. I've already told you it's quite dreadful."

"I'd miss them too." Aiden felt foolish. He was reading things into the conversation, and Jochen's news, that weren't there. Of course their conversations about literature would continue as they had always done. "I'd also miss you, Jochen. You're my closest friend, and I treasure the time we have together."

"Do you trust me, Aiden?"

"What sort of question is that? Of course I trust you." Aiden frowned. "Your question makes it sound as though I shouldn't."

"There was another reason I was late," Jochen said. "It wasn't just because of my acceptance at the university. There's something I want to do with you, for you."

There was something about Jochen's tone that made Aiden nervous. "What?"

"It's not something to talk about first; it's something I need to show you. Finish your tea, and we'll get going." Jochen drained his cup.

"All right." Aiden did as Jochen asked and then followed him out onto the street. It was snowing lightly, fine snowflakes already providing a white blanket across the city. "I hope it's not far. It's cold out here."

"It's not far." Jochen shoved his hands in his pockets as he always did when they were out walking. "This week is the anniversary of when we first met. Do you remember?"

"It's been on my mind."

They were both very different men from that day six years ago. Jochen, too, had changed, although the difference in him was more subtle than in Aiden. But that didn't mean it wasn't noticeable, especially the more time they spent together. Sometimes Aiden felt there was some kind of emptiness in Jochen, a space that needed to be filled somehow. It wasn't obvious, but Aiden had caught him several times wearing a wistful expression, and there was a sadness about him. Aiden hated seeing Jochen like that and wished he knew what to do about it.

He knew from experience that if the emptiness wasn't filled, the nightmares would come. It seemed to invite them in—them and the memories he tried so hard to forget.

That day he'd visited Jochen to the cottage, he'd ended up spending the night in the guest bedroom, as he'd missed the last train back to London. After they'd both retired for the night, Aiden had heard Jochen cry out in his sleep. Heard enough to guess what he was dreaming about.

It was too familiar. In many ways he and Jochen were similar, with the experiences they'd gone through. But where Aiden had allowed the horror of the war to rob him of so much, Jochen hadn't. He admired Jochen for that.

Admired him, but wished like hell he could do something to make Jochen's nightmares go away too.

What the…?

Retreating into his thoughts, Aiden hadn't noticed the direction in which they'd come. He'd focused on Jochen, walking with him, enjoying the companionship.

"We're at the Avery," Aiden said. The theatre was in darkness. It didn't open on Wednesdays. Jochen knew that. It was one of the reasons they met and often made a day of it rather than just meeting for lunch. Fridays' meetings were brief, as Aiden had to get back to the theatre to help get ready for the afternoon and evening performances.

"Yes, we are." Jochen opened the front door and stood back for Aiden to enter.

Aiden frowned. "The door shouldn't be open. We're

closed." He didn't like the theatre when it was closed. He shivered, a chill going down his back. He'd always felt as though the theatre at this time was for ghosts of past performers, those who had once tread the boards and entertained others. They still lurked in the shadows somewhere, and he didn't want to disturb them.

"I... er... I talked to Jack," Jochen said. "The theatre is ours for the afternoon. He's trusting us with it, although I suspect he means he's trusting you more than me."

"Jack said that?" What on earth had Jochen said to Jack? Jack treated his responsibility to the theatre very seriously. Aiden felt fluttering in the base of his stomach, his nervousness building to a sense of dread. "Jochen?" he asked. "What's going on? You're scaring me."

"Please don't be scared." Jochen had such a look of earnestness on his face that Aiden wondered why he had been. "Just trust me. I need you to trust me."

"All right, but I still want to know what's going on." Nevertheless, Aiden followed Jochen through the door that led to backstage. He wasn't about to let Jochen see how he felt. He wouldn't understand how Aiden felt about the empty theatre.

Or maybe he would, and that would be worse. He didn't want Jochen to be scared. Didn't want to see him scared.

However, when Jochen walked onto the stage itself, Aiden froze.

No, no, no.

Jochen turned and held out his hand. "Please, Aiden. You... I... please."

"No." Aiden didn't stand on this stage anymore, and especially not when there was someone else around. He hadn't since that last time Jack had caught him there. He'd been careless and vowed it wouldn't happen again. "What's going on? What are you doing?"

Aiden backed away. He was pale, shaking, and he sounded scared. More than scared. Horrified, angry, and worse than that. Betrayed. Jochen could see it in his eyes.

"Aiden, please." Jochen tried again. Was this too much too fast? He'd seen the difference in Aiden these past few weeks and had hoped—prayed—he was doing the right thing. "This is your stage, where you belong. You need this."

"Need this? What the hell do you know about what I bloody need? Or what I want?" Aiden's voice grew stronger the angrier he became.

Perhaps that was the way to help him? Jochen knew the risk he was taking, that it might destroy his friendship with the one man he truly wanted, but....

Aiden's future was important. If this worked, Aiden could get past everything he'd lost. Did it really matter if Jochen lost everything by doing it?

No, it didn't. Jochen took a deep breath, ready to tell Aiden what he meant to him, to anger him enough to make him react without thinking about his voice.

But before he could say something, Aiden spoke again.

"I can't do this. I'm not the man I was." Despite his words, Aiden edged closer to Jochen, towards the centre of the stage. He laughed, his voice cracking, although it didn't lose anything of its volume. "You wouldn't believe how far away from that man I am now. It's impossible. Everything I want is...."

Aiden stilled and flushed bright red. He looked horrified.

"Everything?" Jochen asked softly. He had to build on this, push Aiden past his limits. It was the only way.

Mrs Hamilton had told him that sometimes one had to be cruel to be kind. But he couldn't do that to Aiden. He'd already gone too far. This had to stop. But neither could he keep lying to Aiden, lying by omission. It wasn't fair. None of this was.

Jochen slipped his hand into Aiden's. Aiden sounded like he had that day they'd first met. There was no hoarseness in his voice at all. "Sing for me. Please."

"I... can't." Aiden didn't let go of Jochen's hand. He didn't run.

That was something.

"Sing *with* me, then. You're not alone, Aiden. I promise you, you're not alone. I'll stay with you for as long as you want me to."

"I want you to stay," Aiden whispered.

Jochen started to sing softly. A Christmas song, as it was that time of year, almost the anniversary of when they'd met. But he didn't sing the same one Aiden had sung six years ago. It didn't seem right. This wasn't about their past. It was time to move forward.

"Silent night, holy night. All is calm, all is bright. Round yon virgin, Mother and Child."

After a few minutes, Aiden joined in softly, but instead of singing in English, his words were in German, his voice gradually getting stronger. "*Holder Knabe im lockigen Haar, Schlaf in himmlischer Ruh.*"

"Sleep in heavenly peace." By the time Jochen sang the final line of the verse, they were singing a duet, different words but the same meaning. Aiden's voice was strong and clear as Jochen remembered it.

Except this time it wasn't a memory. It was real. Not just his reality, but theirs.

They both stopped singing and smiled at each other.

"I'll tell you what *I* want, Aiden," Jochen said. "You." He kissed Aiden, not on the forehead, but on the mouth so there would be no doubt about his meaning. Despite that, the kiss was brief, and as chaste as Jochen could be, as much as he wanted more.

"That's what I want too. You, I mean. I want you." Aiden returned the kiss, but his was lingering and sweet.

Everything Jochen had thought Aiden kissing him would be, and more. Aiden wanted this. He really wanted this too.

Jochen brushed his fingers against Aiden's cheek. They'd already wasted so much time. "I didn't... I thought... I've wanted to do that for so long," Jochen said.

"So have I."

They both leaned in for another kiss. The duet they had sung, this celebration of music, wasn't just their present, but the beginning of their future.

Together.

EPILOGUE

"Penny for them," Aiden said softly. He threaded his fingers through Jochen's hair, smiling when Jochen leaned into his touch.

Aiden sat on the floor, his back against the couch. Jochen had positioned himself between Aiden's legs, his head resting on Aiden's chest. He'd worried about it hurting Aiden's injured leg, but Aiden had assured him it didn't. His leg only protested if he put his weight on it for extended periods of time, and he enjoyed being close with Jochen like this.

"I wasn't thinking that loudly," Jochen protested, "and keep doing that, although I'll have to get up soon and put more wood on the fire."

"The fire can die down a bit more before you have to move." Aiden sighed contentedly. He loved the afternoons they spent together at Lavender Cottage. It was a safe haven for both of them—somewhere they could enjoy each other's company properly without worrying about being caught. "Another couple of hours and I'll need to catch the train back to London."

Jochen sat up and shuffled along so he was sitting next to Aiden. "What if you didn't have to?"

Aiden frowned. "I have to go back to London, Jochen. It's where I live. You know I can't stay here."

He often found himself thinking back to that day a few months ago at the Avery Theatre. Aiden had not only found his voice, but discovered that the feelings he'd had for Jochen were reciprocated.

Even so, they'd taken their relationship slowly. Some exploring and touching in front of the fire, and kissing of course. Aiden loved kissing Jochen. He tasted wonderful, his lips moist, and his scent—Aiden couldn't describe it, but had decided it embodied everything he'd come to think of as this man he loved. Gentle, yet strong. Caring and passionate. Jochen had told Aiden that it was fine if Aiden preferred to take things slowly. He was content with what they had, and they had the rest of their lives for their relationship to grow into whatever they wanted it to be.

At least in private. No matter how they felt about each other, they could never be a couple anywhere else.

If someone caught them together like this, they'd both be thrown into prison, or worse. No one suspected their true feelings for each other, and that was the way it needed to stay.

Jochen kissed Aiden softly and took his hand. When he spoke, his German accent was stronger than usual—it grew thicker when he was emotional. "I want you to be the last person I see when I close my eyes at night, and the first I see in the morning. I'm not suggesting we tell anyone about our relationship." He swallowed. "I might be an idiot at times, but I'm not crazy or suicidal."

"You're not an idiot, Jochen." Aiden squeezed Jochen's hand. "You're one of the most intelligent men I've ever met, even if you are an incurable romantic at times. But I like that about you. I love it when you read poetry to me, even when it's not in English. The sound of your voice carries me with it, like a pebble on the tide."

"A wintertide," Jochen said, referring to a Tennyson poem they both loved. It was apt, considering the thick snow outside. "It's not my intention to suggest something you'd be uncomfortable with, but on days such as this, I do worry about you navigating the snow on your way home."

"That's very sweet, my love, but—"

"The cottage has a spare room. You've used it before on the odd occasion." Jochen interrupted before Aiden could speak further. "It's quite acceptable for two bachelors to move in together. You've often said that you can't stay at Mrs Hamilton's forever."

"It was only ever meant to be temporary," Aiden agreed. He'd lived there for much longer than he'd originally intended, but Mrs Hamilton wouldn't hear of him moving out when he wasn't ready to do so, and he'd never considered it until now. For so many years, he'd clung to his routines like a lifeline. Being with Jochen had given him the courage—and desire—to finally start living again. Besides, she liked Jochen and had confided in Aiden that she was beginning to consider him as family. After all, Jochen had no family of his own in England, so *someone* had to take care of him. "Wait a minute. You expect me to move into your *spare room*?"

"Ah, yes." Jochen chuckled at the disbelief in Aiden's voice. Aiden couldn't tell if he was teasing or not. "Did you have something else in mind?"

"Are you asking me to share your bed?" Aiden asked quietly. Surely that was what Jochen meant? Or had he got it completely wrong? Oh hell. Heat rushed to his face. "I...

that *was* what you meant, wasn't it?" He tried to lighten his tone, but was too aware of the familiar hoarseness trying to edge its way back in. "I'd be happy in your spare room too. I...." He trailed off, mortified.

It was difficult enough having to leave at the end of each visit knowing he would have a lonely night ahead of him. Knowing Jochen was on the other side of the wall—he wasn't sure he could do it.

"Yes, that was what I meant, and.... You *want* to sleep in the spare room?" Jochen looked as horrified at the idea as Aiden felt. "Of course if that's what you want, that's fine," he added, although Aiden knew him well enough to know it wasn't really.

"No," Aiden said quickly. "I don't want to sleep in the spare room." He swallowed, wishing they'd made another pot of tea, as his throat felt suddenly as dry as sandpaper.

"Good." Jochen sounded relieved. "But that's what we'll have to tell everyone of course. You'd have to keep your belongings there, so it looks lived in. Everyone in the village knows you love it here, and they keep asking when you're coming to visit next, so I doubt they'll be surprised that you've decided to stay. Mary at the pub says you have quite the colour in your cheeks now compared to the first time she met you." He stopped to catch his breath, his babbling a sure sign he was nervous.

"You've been talking about me with Mary?"

"She's been talking to me about you," Jochen corrected. He grew silent, his attention taken by the waning flames of the fire in front of them. "I've found a home here at Lavender Cottage, Aiden, but it only really feels like it when we're here together. I'll keep you safe. I promise. I'd never put you in danger. I love you."

"Yes," Aiden said.

"Yes?" Jochen looked up at Aiden, puzzled. "Yes, what? Yes, you know I love you, or that I'll keep you safe?"

Aiden smiled. "Yes, I know, but more than that, yes, I'll move in." He linked their fingers together. "I wish we didn't have to hide what we have, but as long as I don't have to hide how I feel with you, that will be enough. I've spent so many years hiding, Jochen, not just from life but from myself. I don't want to do it again. I need somewhere, someone with whom I can be myself. I need you, but more than that, I *love* you."

"Stay with me tonight," Jochen whispered. "I need that too." He leaned into Aiden, their foreheads touching. "The snow's getting heavy out there. We can telephone Mrs Hamilton so she doesn't worry."

"You're right, it is, and it would be foolish to venture out in it tonight," Aiden said. "Come on, I'll help you bring in more wood for the fire. It's going to be a long night. I'm very much looking forward to it."

CONNECT WITH ANNE

Contact me at
darthanne@gmail.com
annebarwell.wordpress.com

Anne Barwell lives in Wellington, New Zealand. She shares her home with Kaylee: a cat with "tortitude" who is convinced that the house is run to suit her; this is an ongoing "discussion," and to date, it appears as though Kaylee may be winning.

In 2008, Anne completed her conjoint BA in English Literature and Music/Bachelor of Teaching. She has worked as a music teacher, a primary school teacher, and now works in a library. She is a member of the Upper Hutt Science Fiction Club and plays violin for Hutt Valley Orchestra.

She is an avid reader across a wide range of genres and a watcher of far too many TV series and movies, although it can be argued that there is no such thing as "too many." These, of course, are best enjoyed with a decent cup of tea and further the continuing argument that the concept of "spare time" is really just a myth. She also hosts and reviews for other authors, and writes monthly blog posts for Love Bytes. She is the co-founder of the New Zealand Rainbow Romance writers, and a member of RWNZ.

Anne's books have received honourable mentions five times, reached the finals four times—one of which was for best gay book—and been a runner up in the Rainbow Awards. She has also been nominated twice in the Goodreads M/M Romance Reader's Choice Awards—once for Best Fantasy and once for Best Historical.

www.ingramcontent.com/pod-product-compliance
Lightning Source LLC
Chambersburg PA
CBHW071925130726
47909CB00014B/2587